Sardines

SASHI KAUFMAN

Quill Tree Books
An Imprint of HarperCollinsPublishers

Quill Tree Books is an imprint of HarperCollins Publishers.

Sardines

Copyright © 2022 by Sashi Kaufman

All rights reserved. Printed in the United States of America.

No part of this book may be used or reproduced in any manner
whatsoever without written permission except in the case of
brief quotations embodied in critical articles and reviews. For
information address HarperCollins Children's Books, a division of
HarperCollins Publishers, 195 Broadway, New York, NY 10007.
www.harpercollinschildrens.com

Library of Congress Control Number: 2022937883
ISBN 978-0-06-299561-2

Typography by Kathy H. Lam
22 23 24 25 26   PC/LSCH   10 9 8 7 6 5 4 3 2 1

First Edition

FOR ELIANA AND AVI

🐟 🐟 🐟

CHAPTER 1

THE THING ABOUT A NEW SCHOOL YEAR IS IT'S NOT NEW.
Not in any of the ways that matter. Getting off the bus, still
wearing last year's sneakers and a T-shirt that was getting
tight in the armpits, I was uncomfortably the same. But
I had a few hopes for Feltzer Harding Regional Middle
School. Sixth grade was not elementary school. We had
new things like homeroom and health class, and you could
order à la carte in the cafeteria if you brought money and
only wanted to eat cookies and Doritos for lunch. We
each had our own schedule. Mine had arrived over the
summer, and I had read it over and over again until I had
it practically memorized. And the smell that seemed to
haunt elementary school, of old construction paper and

watered-down glue, was replaced by a mix of industrial cleaner and Axe body spray.

There were new kids, too. Sixty kids from the elementary school one town over and the sixty kids from our school were smooshed together into one grade. As we got off our buses, they got off their buses on the opposite side of the bus circle. I wondered for a minute if each one of us had an exact counterpart coming off the other bus. I looked sideways at the kids from Keyser Falls. I scanned their faces, looking for another not-too-tall, not-too-short white kid with brown hair and blue eyes. But no one matched.

Mom said, "Never compare your insides to other people's outsides," but it was hard when everyone else's outsides had new sneakers and backpacks and clothes with that creased off-the-hanger look. Their faces looked excited and happy.

We all milled around in front of the school, waiting for the bell to ring and the doors to open. I stared down at my feet, aware that the kids around me were all greeting each other, talking about camp and going to the beach, and getting out their schedules to see if they had any classes together. I stared up at the flagpole, pretending to be concerned about the way the corner was folded in and stuck around one of the metal grommets. I didn't want to be that kid who looked like he was looking around for someone to talk to. It was one thing to feel lonely; it was another thing when everyone knew it.

"Hey, Lucas," came a friendly voice. It was Robbie Belcher. He smiled, showing off a mouth full of new metal hardware. "How was your summer?"

"Okay," I lied. "How about you?"

Robbie shrugged. "Okay, until this. I just got them on last week, and my mouth is so sore it's like throttling."

"You mean throbbing?"

"Yeah, I guess so." He pulled a medicine bottle out of his pocket and shook it so the pills rattled. "My mom gave me this to give to the school nurse in case my teeth are bothering me."

I nodded, and then we stood there. I didn't know what else to say. Robbie and I had gone to aftercare together since kindergarten, but he was the kind of kid who was nice to pretty much everyone, so I was never sure if I could count him as an actual friend. Still, if you had to be alone, it was better to be alone with someone else.

Finally, a man in a short-sleeve white dress shirt with serious pit stains came out, introduced himself as the assistant principal, and yelled a bunch of things that I don't think anyone could hear. Maybe it was a welcome speech; maybe he was telling us that the bathrooms were all flooded and unusable. Even if the wind hadn't been drowning him out, I wouldn't have been able to hear him. There was a group of kids in front of me with Greg Hutchins at the center. Greg wasn't even pretending to pay attention to what the assistant principal was saying. He had his back toward him and was talking loudly, surrounded by a bunch of boys who all wore variations of the same uniform: sports shorts, T-shirts, and baseball hats. I recognized some of them from elementary school. Some of them were new faces—same look, though—drawn right to Greg like a bunch of mosquitoes to a warm, fleshy cow butt.

When we finally got to file into school, the assistant principal pointed right at Greg and pulled him out of the crowd. I couldn't hear what he said, but the finger kept pointing, and the tops of Greg's ears got red.

I followed the crush of kids into the lobby, but I kept my eyes down as we passed in front of the glass trophy cases. I knew what I would see there. I had seen it on Step Up Day when our eighth-grade tour guide stopped there to show off the school trophies for everything from basketball and football to math team and the state geography bee. On a special shelf were pictures of every student who had ever won the Principal's Award for All-Around Attitude, Effort, and Achievement at Feltzer Harding Middle School. And there, shining out at me, in full color, his dirty-blond hair falling partially in his eyes, was the eighth-grade version of my brother.

Any teacher I ever had who'd had Charlie too—and that was most of them because our town was so small—practically fell out of their seat when I told them that, yes, I was related to *that* Charlie Barnes. And for the first week or so I could do no wrong. But then, slowly, the shine would rub off. I couldn't keep up, even with his memory.

Charlie was nine years older, so I was in preschool when he was in sixth grade at Feltzer Harding Middle School. When he went off to college, I was only in fourth grade. Less than a year later he was dead.

I learned a lot in fifth grade, but none of it was school stuff. I learned that there are worse things than being the younger brother of an all-star kid like Charlie Barnes. I learned what adults mean when they say "spotty attendance." And I learned that even when you stick out for something, it's still possible to feel like you are completely invisible.

CHAPTER 2

"SORRY, KIDS, THE FIRST DAY OF SCHOOL IS A LOT OF paperwork," Mrs. Lynch, my new homeroom teacher, said as she passed out about a thousand different forms. "I know some of you are pretty upset about not jumping right into learning," she said, and winked at us. Mrs. Lynch had that seasoned-teacher look: a bunch of pencils sticking out of her bun and a giant coffee mug steaming on her desk. She helped us sort all the papers into two piles: things that had to come back with a signature and things that would go home and stay home.

"This is the most important one," Mrs. Lynch said, holding up Sadie Gillespie's double-sided parent contact and information sheet. I flipped mine over, relieved to see that Mom's information was still on it. Not that it would do anyone any good. Mom hadn't answered her phone since she left three weeks ago—not even for Dad. I knew because I heard him cursing about it when he thought I was in the shower.

I stared down at the even lines of formal print, thinking about how even their detailed contact information didn't have the answers I wanted. Dad worked for a heating and insulation company, and Mom was a waitress at Townline Diner. Mom had listed Dad's parents as a backup contact even though I hadn't seen or heard from them, except for a card at Christmas, since Charlie died. The other emergency contact was Mom's friend, and boss at the diner, Rosie. There had better not be any emergencies that Dad couldn't handle, because there wasn't much left for backup.

I stuffed the papers into my bag and half listened as Mrs. Lynch went over the bell schedule for the first day and assigned us lockers. Robbie had the locker next to mine, since they were assigned alphabetically and Belcher came right after Barnes. I stuck my empty backpack in, and watched as Robbie unloaded new notebooks, pencils, highlighters, and index cards, all still in their plastic wrapping. He shrugged sheepishly. "My mom likes to get this stuff as soon as she gets the list."

"I didn't know there was a list," I mumbled.

"I think they emailed it to us," Robbie said.

Right. No home computer at our house. No mom, no phone. No phone, no email. Dad had a phone, but he only used it for calling and maybe texting. He always said the rest of it was just a way to waste time. I swallowed hard on the sadness rising in the back of my throat.

That was it for homeroom and English class with Mrs. Lynch. Robbie and I had different math classes, so we went our separate ways. "I'll see you at lunch?" he said hopefully. I nodded, not even trying to conceal my relief.

Most years I had new stuff too. Mom and I went to Walmart every year on the Saturday before school started, and she'd let me pick out a couple of new shirts with my school supplies. Then we would go to the diner where she worked and sit at the counter, and I could order anything I wanted for lunch. But this year Mom was gone, and Dad didn't know about any of that—not that he would have done anything anyway. So not only was *I* not new, I didn't even have the illusion of being new—even if it did wear off by lunchtime.

I didn't say much of anything to anyone in my classes. Some kids I knew from elementary school, but some were strangers from the other school. I sat down in my assigned seat and tried hard to listen to the teacher talking. Anything to avoid the way my brain was empty and buzzing like a fluorescent light that's about to die. When we played a getting-to-know-you game in gym class, I couldn't come up with a favorite ice cream flavor or an animal that started with the same letter as my first name. I wanted to scream, *Who cares? My mom is gone! Isn't anyone going to do anything about it?*

And then Anna Perkins, probably the prettiest girl in the whole sixth grade, whispered, "Lemur." And I almost cried. Because "lemur" was basically the nicest thing anyone had said to me in a month. And there was something about the way she said it that made me think she could see how cruddy I was feeling and felt bad for me, in a good way.

The cafeteria was big and loud. Everyone sat down at tables like they knew where they were supposed to go. I actually looked around for a seating chart because it seemed like maybe I had missed something. Last year everyone had talked about how awesome middle school was going to be and how we could do so much more stuff on our own, but actually it was kind of terrifying to be left on your own to figure stuff out. Finally, after wandering around in a circle with my tray and being told by a teacher on duty to "just find a seat," I found Robbie sitting with a bunch of boys at a round table in the back. A couple of them I recognized, like Cory Kepperman, who I knew had been in Robbie's class last year. Two others were wearing the same Little League hat as Robbie, so I figured that was how he knew them. I sighed loudly as I finally sank down into an empty chair.

"You okay?" Robbie said.

"Yeah," I said. "This place is loud."

"Food looks decent, though," Robbie said, pointing toward my chicken burger and tater tots.

I glanced over at his lunch box, which was overflowing with a sandwich, chips, and cut-up fruit, all packed in neat little containers. There was a handwritten note with a SpongeBob sticker on it poking out of the top but when Robbie saw me looking, he blushed and stuffed it back in his bag. "That's Jack Thomas and Peter Kapinsky," he said, pointing to the two kids in the matching hats. Robbie pointed to his own hat and grinned. "We thought it would be cool to all wear them on the first day of school." Jack Thomas scowled at Robbie, as if to point out that trying for cool was pretty much the least cool thing you could do in middle school, but if Robbie noticed or cared, it didn't seem like it.

"What do you have after lunch?" he asked.

"Science."

"Me too! With who?" he asked, pulling his crumpled schedule out of his pocket.

"Ms. Edgerly," I said. I didn't need to check.

Ms. Edgerly had been Charlie's favorite teacher. He talked about her all the time. I even think it used to make Dad a little jealous how much Charlie looked up to her. And that was saying something, because when it came to showing emotion, Dad was like one of those British soldiers with the tall hats who guard the palace.

According to Charlie, Ms. Edgerly was the "most chill" teacher ever. First of all, she didn't believe in homework, and her class was actually interesting—Charlie said that was what got him to like science. She did all these cool labs and hands-on projects. I remember this paper roller coaster that was in Charlie's room forever. He used to let me drop marbles down it and watch them roll through the chutes. Even when he was in high school, Charlie used to go back and see Ms. Edgerly all the time.

After lunch Robbie and I walked over to her room and took our seats. Ms. Edgerly's room was different from the other classes I'd been in. She kept the overhead lights off and had a bunch of different lamps set up around the room. There was a huge fish tank that was attached to something called a living machine. The whole thing made a humming, gurgling noise that was kind of soothing. When she called attendance, I waited eagerly for her to get to my name. I had a smile prepared: a small one, not like I was sucking up. But when she said my name out loud and looked over at me, she grimaced, and a crease formed between her eyebrows. Then she looked right back down. And I felt like a real jerk just sitting there with this stupid grin on my face.

After that I didn't have too many more expectations for middle school.

CHAPTER 3

MRS. LYNCH CAUGHT MY SLEEVE AS I STARTED TO SHUFFLE
out to the bus line at the end of the day. "You're Lucas,
right? You're not on my bus list."

I turned red. "Oh, I thought all the bus students went
at the same time."

"They do. But I've got you down for the Teen Club
after-school program."

I could have sworn I heard Greg Hutchins snickering as
he walked past. "I'm not supposed to be. I mean, my mom
signed me up, but then she changed her mind." I wasn't
going to tell her that we agreed it wasn't really something
we could afford, and I could most likely survive at home by
myself until her shift was over or Dad got home from work.

Mrs. Lynch twisted her lips as she stared down at the piece of paper that told her where each student was supposed to go. "Well, do you want to check in at the office? Until I hear from them, I really can't let you get on the bus."

I nodded and walked down to the office, where a very nice, apple-cheeked lady told me that Mom hadn't made any changes to my schedule. "But I can call her, and we can clear it up right now over the phone," she offered.

The first week Mom was gone, I called her phone and left messages. At first I kept calm, but by the second week I couldn't keep the panic and the whining out of my voice. Where was she? Why wouldn't she return my calls? By the third week, her voicemail was full, and it had been ever since.

"I'll talk to her later," I lied, and then walked down to the cafeteria to see what middle school aftercare had in store for me. Inside the cafeteria a custodian was pushing a collection of milk cartons and plastic baggies in front of an enormous broom. Someone had tacked up a poster-sized sign that said *Teen Club* over the menu board, but otherwise everything looked pretty much the same. I mean, who were we kidding? Aftercare in middle school was just a half step away from juvenile prison. An exasperated woman named Andrea was already going through the rules in a voice that held not even the faintest whiff of back-to-school excitement.

"The first half hour is homework time. If you have homework, you need to do homework. If you don't have homework, you need to read. If you need to go to the bathroom, you have to ask. Everyone gets one snack. There's no talking during homework time. If you're going to work together on your homework, you need to have a note from your teacher. After homework time it's outside time. We all go outside as long as it's above thirty degrees. Once we go outside, you can't come back inside until outside time is over. Outside time is on the tar." Here she paused and took a breath. "No one goes off the tar!"

I glanced outside just to confirm that there wasn't any boiling hot lava just south of the tar, but all I saw was some tired-looking grass mixed with gravel. I looked around at the other members of Teen Club. It seemed there were four of us considered too defective to stay home alone without licking batteries or blowing up the microwave. Robbie was there, along with Anna Perkins and a serious-looking girl from the other elementary school who wore a basketball sweatshirt and introduced herself as Cat.

Since it was the first day of school, we didn't actually have any homework, something that Andrea seemed to hold against us. We ate our snack of graham crackers and milk and then stared at her as she stared back at us. Finally, she grudgingly allowed us to go outside early. Not that outside was a whole lot better.

It turned out Andrea was afraid of ticks—all bugs, really, but especially ticks. We weren't allowed to put even one toe onto the grass that bordered the parking lot, much less go anywhere near the woods beyond it. There was a faded four-square court painted on one corner of the parking lot and a netless basketball hoop that leaned to one side. Never mind that the only ball we had was a half-deflated soccer ball. So we milled around for the required outdoor period like convicts in a prison yard. Robbie and I walked side by side for a while, kicking at a chunk of tar. "I'm not even supposed to be here," I said. "My mom and I decided—" I started to say but quickly stopped, realizing that Robbie might ask questions I didn't have answers to.

"My mom is ridiculously overprotective. You know what she had on the table this morning at breakfast? My DARE pledge! You know—that paper we all signed last year, not to do drugs. I was like, 'Mom, you know I'm going to middle school, not New York City!'" He laughed and shook his head. "Anyway, this isn't so bad. If I was home, I'd probably have to watch my sister and brothers, or fight with them over the Xbox. At least here we get to hang out with friends." I glanced around quickly, wondering if I'd missed somebody. On the other side of the tar Cat was staring up at the tilted basketball hoop like it was a problem she had to solve. Anna was standing next to her, but they didn't look like they were talking. Something under my ribs relaxed a little bit when I realized he was talking about me.

We shared the parking lot with younger kids who were bused over from the other elementary school for after-school supervision. They had their own babysitter, a woman named Louise who sat in a lawn chair wrapped up to her eyeballs in a fleece Patriots blanket even though it was September. The younger kids seemed to have no problem with the limited space and played endless games of tag and Red Rover.

Around four thirty everyone started to get picked up by parents who always looked tired and only sometimes looked happy to see them. Whoever was left at five thirty joined the line filing back in past Andrea, who stared at us and asked individually as we passed if we had our belongings and if we had checked for ticks. I thought I might know a bit about how immigrants at Ellis Island had felt upon arriving in our country. I'm sure Andrea wouldn't have hesitated to chemically delouse us if she could.

Dad was the last one to pick up. I could feel Andrea's eyes boring holes into me as the big black hands of the clock clicked toward five thirty, then five forty-five, and finally almost six o'clock. When I saw Dad's dark green truck pull into the bus circle, I jumped up and practically sprinted for the door. When I climbed into the passenger side, he was on the phone, arguing with someone about work.

"I told you, that's the way the closet was when we got there. Yeah? Well I'm not going back over there. I'm not a handyman, for God's sake." Then he said "yeah" a few more times, hung up the phone, and tossed it behind him into the back seat. I waited awhile, hoping he would ask me about my day, but then he turned on the radio, and I could tell by the way he squinted his eyes that he was still thinking about the phone call.

When we turned into the driveway of Oak Hill Trailer Park, he turned and looked at me like he'd just all of a sudden noticed I was there. "First day go okay?" he asked.

"Yeah, I guess so."

Dad nodded.

"I don't need to go to aftercare. Mom and I agreed that I could stay home by myself in the afternoons now. And it's expensive." I added this last part not sure of how it would go over. On the one hand, Dad was aware that we didn't have a lot of money. On the other hand, he didn't like to be reminded about it. The squinty-eyed face came back. I knew right away I should have waited until after we'd gotten home and he had a beer.

"You and Mom decided this, huh?"

"Yeah."

"Well, things are different now."

I didn't have a response for that. After Charlie died, Mom, Dad, and I were like a three-legged table: still standing but maybe not super stable. Without Mom, we weren't much of anything: just a bunch of broken parts stuck together by the whirring motion of our daily lives.

"Besides," Dad went on, "we *can* afford it, and it's easy for me to pick you up on the way home. Maybe . . ." But here he trailed off without finishing the sentence.

"Maybe when Mom comes back?"

Dad glared at me. He pulled into the driveway and got out of the car without answering me. "You said three weeks," I added. I was really digging a hole now. But it was like I couldn't stop myself. Like whatever feelings I'd stuffed down all day at school were coming up in the back of my throat, bitter and acidic. "I don't know why she can't even call." And then, because he wasn't answering me anymore,

I added to the back of his head as he walked slowly up the wooden steps of the porch in front of our trailer, "Is she ever coming back?"

Dad turned around. I had been trying to make him mad in one way or another, but instead he just looked at me sadly, shrugged his shoulders, and said, "I don't know."

Later that night Dad sent me out to bring in the trash cans. There were two rows of trailer homes on either side of the main driveway through the park. Most of them were single-wides like ours. Dad called those semi-perms, like semipermanent. There were a few travel trailers but even those had squishy half-deflated wheels or tarps thrown over them to protect against the weather. Mr. Boudreau, our landlord, was out trying to wrangle a lid and bungee cord with his one good arm. I wasn't sure exactly what was wrong with the other one, but it just kind of dangled out of his sleeve and didn't seem to do much. He and his wife were the only other year-round residents of Oak Hill Trailer Park. The garbage truck only picked up out front, so I usually helped him out on trash night and he paid me a couple of bucks or a candy bar or something.

"Hey, Lucas!" he said brightly when he saw me. "You know what I did today?"

I shook my head.

"A hole in one on the windmill!"

The windmill was a tricky hole at the Clams Casino mini-golf course in York Beach. Mr. Boudreau was obsessed with mini golf. I guess he had been a regular golfer before he hurt his arm. Now mini golf was his passion. He knew every course between Kittery and Portland, including the dates they would close for the season. When his grandkids came to visit, he'd even take me with them for a round or two.

I helped him secure the lid on the trash can and then dragged two more cans back toward the brick patio in front of his double-wide. The Boudreaus had the nicest home at Oak Hill. Mrs. Boudreau really liked to garden, and she had planted a whole bunch of vines that crept up the sides and had flowers on them.

"First day of school today?" Mr. Boudreau asked.

"Yeah," I said, flatly.

"That good?"

"It was okay," I said.

"It will get better," Mr. Boudreau said, and then he looked at me kind of intently. "Hey, I don't think I paid you last week," he added, reaching into his pocket and handing me a five-dollar bill.

I hesitated. "I think you did."

"Well, it's a back-to-school bonus, then," he said, and smiled.

I took the money and turned back toward our trailer, rolling the trash can behind me.

"Hey, Lucas," Mr. Boudreau called. "You think we could build something like that windmill here? Maybe a mini course all our own? Make a little attraction out of it. Ask your dad what he thinks."

I nodded and smiled. It was Mr. Boudreau's dream to have an in-house mini-golf course as part of Oak Hill Trailer Park. I didn't have the heart to tell him that whatever Dad dreamed of, I was pretty sure it didn't involve mini-golf courses.

CHAPTER 4

THE FIRST WEEK OF SCHOOL IS AWKWARD, BUT THE second week of school has to be the worst time to be a new kid. The week before, everyone was new, but in the second week you have to do the whole new-kid thing and have all your teachers introduce you to everyone. Just the thought of it made me sweat. So when our math teacher announced that we were getting a new kid, I winced before I even looked up. Then I saw him and winced some more and looked back down at my shoes.

"Welcome, Phineas Clark," Miss LeGage said brightly. She was a first-year teacher (something you should probably never tell your students) who so far seemed to alternate between being totally overexcited about things like fractions and totally terrified by the fire drill we'd had last week. She got so worked up as we walked out of school into the parking lot, I thought maybe the school really was about to go up in flames.

Phineas Clark stood in front of the class beaming like he'd just won a prize. His navy-blue polo shirt was buttoned up to the very top and tucked into his khaki pants. No one wore khakis, or, for that matter, a belt, like the braided leather one holding up his pants. I glanced over at Greg Hutchins, wondering if this kid would get picked on before or after he sat down on his very first day. But Phineas Clark was lucky, because Greg wasn't even paying attention. Instead he was jabbing his pencil into something that was stuck to the bottom of his desk.

"Do you prefer Phineas or Finn?" Miss LeGage asked him.

"Finn, I suppose, though either will do," he said neatly.

Now Greg's head shot up. He glanced at one of his minions sitting next to him and made a face. I knew that face. This kid was in trouble. I glanced quickly away as Miss LeGage directed him to the only open seat, which was, of course, right next to me. "Lucas, can you show our new student where we are in the textbook? I'm sure he'll get his own by this afternoon."

He executed a little bow in her direction before taking his seat.

I pushed my open book to the edge of my desk so he could look on, to which he responded, "Thank you, my good man."

The girl who sat in front of us nudged her friend and they both started giggling, but Finn merely smiled at her and turned his attention forward. He didn't have any notebooks or paper, just a pen shaped like a miniature wooden baseball bat, which he played with all during class.

After class I followed him at a distance and watched as he pretended to tip his imaginary cap—hats were allowed only at lunchtime—at passing teachers and once at the principal, Mrs. Donahue. When he stopped at the water fountain, he drank, then gargled, then drank some more, and smacked his lips at the end like it was the best water he'd ever tasted. Was it confidence or insanity? I wanted to know, but I was also afraid to get too close.

"There's a new kid," I told Robbie at lunch.

"Really?" asked Robbie excitedly. "Is he cool? Should we ask him to sit with us?" He half stood up in his seat, scanning the cafeteria.

"No!" I said, maybe a little too forcefully. "I mean, our table's full anyway. Besides, I think Greg Hutchins has his eye on him already."

"Oh," Robbie said soberly, his face dropping. "Well, maybe tomorrow.

"Hey," Robbie said to our table, "I got a new Minecraft Lego set from my grandparents. It looks really awesome, but my mom says I have to wait for a rainy day to start it. Lucas is like a true Lego master," Robbie told Cory, Peter, and Jack. Only Cory looked vaguely interested in this information, but Robbie just kept on talking. "Remember that project you did in like third grade?"

Everyone had been assigned a town building to re-create as part of a model we were making as a class. I was absent the day we got to pick our buildings, so I ended up being assigned the town transfer station.

"It was the dump!" Robbie exclaimed. "And he built the whole thing out of Legos."

"Isn't that just a bunch of piles of trash?" Jack Thomas asked skeptically.

"Yeah," Robbie said, "but he made all the things in the piles out of Legos: old mattresses, boxes, furniture, scrap metal. And there were buildings, too. It was the coolest."

I appreciated Robbie's enthusiasm, but I was beginning to question his definition of *cool*.

I didn't see Finn anywhere at lunch, but he turned up at Teen Club, bringing our number from four to five. Andrea looked at him with annoyance, as if the presence of one more kid was throwing off her plans for the afternoon. But Finn just smiled at her and took a seat. He seemed extra pleased with our snack, which was weird, because it was orange juice in one of those tiny plastic containers and cheesy goldfish crackers, which didn't really go together except that they were both orange.

Finn didn't do his homework during homework time. Instead he fiddled endlessly with his baseball-bat pen. He had a lot of tricks he could do with that pen. He could twist it between his fingers and balance it on his thumb. He liked to wiggle it and make it look like it was a wobbly noodle. It seemed to have a natural home in the palm of his hand, and all the lacquer was worn off in the places where his fingers gripped it. Watching Finn was more interesting than doing our homework, and pretty soon that's what we were all doing instead. Andrea stared at him, and I could tell she was trying to think of a reason to take the pen away, but he really wasn't doing anything that conflicted with one of the five thousand rules she'd told us about on the first day.

"I was new last year," Anna volunteered shyly. "My stepdad is in the Coast Guard, so we move a lot." She gave a small smile, which made a dimple appear in her left cheek.

"Seafaring folk!" Finn said brightly.

"Sort of," Anna said. "He's an electrical engineer, so sometimes he fixes stuff on the boats. But we don't actually ride on them." Anna hung out with the popular kids, but I'd never seen her gang up and be mean to other kids the way they sometimes did. I guess being new, and one of the only Black kids in our town, she was kind of an outsider too.

"Where did you move from?" she asked.

"Just up the road apiece," Finn said vaguely.

"Did your old school suck as much as this one does?" Cat asked.

Finn pondered the question for a moment before answering, "I think each middle school is a unique cultural amalgam of learning and the dynamic metamorphosis of puberty."

"Wow," said Robbie as a goldfish fell from his open mouth onto the table. "Do you always talk like that?" Coming from anyone else it might have sounded mean, but Robbie sounded genuinely curious.

"I suppose I do take pleasure in a certain verbal gymnastics."

Cat shrugged and went back to filling out her vocabulary worksheet.

🐟 🐟 🐟

A couple of weeks later Andrea wasn't there and in her place was a much younger guy who introduced himself as Steve. Andrea, he told us, had been called up to work in the main office for community services. We were all curious about him, but no one could think of anything to ask. Finally, Cat stood up and asked to go to the bathroom. Steve, who appeared to be playing a game on his phone, waved her off with his hand.

"So, I can go?" she asked, pulling nervously on the strings of the Duke Basketball sweatshirt she wore almost every day.

He looked up from his phone. "Sure. It's right there, isn't it?" He pointed through the double doors of the cafeteria to where the student bathrooms were located. We all nodded back. "Doesn't look too dangerous," he said, and went back to his phone.

A few minutes later, Finn got up from his seat. "Can *I* go?" he asked, pointing toward the double doors.

Steve put down his phone and looked at him quizzically. "Do you guys always ask? You're what? Eleven? Twelve?" We nodded. "Old enough to go the bathroom without asking, right?"

We hesitated. Was this a trick question? We were still

technically in school. During class you had to sign out in your planner *and* on the clipboard by the door, and some teachers even made you carry a bathroom pass like Mr. Connolly's fuzzy green parrot or Mrs. Robertson's fake femur bone, each probably carrying enough bacteria to collapse civilization. "Right," Finn said, and he strode off toward the boys' room. We all watched him. Even Anna, who usually did her homework like she was being timed, pausing only to change the song on her phone.

Anna was the only one of us who had her own phone. Her mother used it to tell her when she was exactly six minutes away from the school so that Anna would be ready and meet her at the door. On the rare occasion Mrs. Perkins actually came in, she barely looked up from her own phone to beckon Anna toward her. She wore a suit—the only one of our parents who did—and she had some kind of important job at a bank. I assumed this because her shiny black car had a license plate with *BANKR* on it. She did not look like the type of person who liked her time to be wasted.

I'd heard one of the other girls in my class say that Anna looked like Rihanna, so I'd googled her once to see what they were talking about. I guess there was a little resemblance. They both had tawny brown skin and green eyes, but honestly, I thought Anna was prettier. She wore her curly black hair in tight braids around her face, but behind her ears it poofed out in a series of springy ringlets. As far as I could tell, almost everybody in Springfield, Maine, was white, so I bet that Anna got stared at a lot. Mostly I liked the face of concentration Anna had while she did her homework. She bit her lower lip and rested the eraser of her pencil right between her eyebrows. She did this the most when she did math. She must have been in the advanced class, because the stuff she was doing looked really complicated.

That first day we went outside with Steve, I could tell Finn was planning something. Steve barely looked up from his phone even when the soccer ball scuttered off into the grass and Finn went to chase it down. Where the pavement ended there was a sloping hill of grass, mostly brown and faded yellow in late September. At the bottom of the hill the grass ended and the woods began. There were trails through the woods. I knew some kids who walked through them to get to school. Finn took his time coming back, slowly kicking the ball in front of him and dragging his feet.

"Hey!" Louise yelled at him from her lawn chair. But Steve just looked up for a second and said nothing.

Finn kicked the ball back to the younger kids and then walked slowly but purposefully over to Steve. "Can we go in there?" he asked, pointing toward the woods.

Steve looked up as if he were seeing the trees and bushes for the first time. He shrugged. "Sure," he said. "But don't go too far."

I heard Louise cough in that way that grown-ups do when they need to talk to each other where kids can't hear, but I was already walking toward the trees. We all were. Following Finn into the woods.

CHAPTER 5

WHEN WE WALKED DOWN THE SLOPING LAWN, AWAY FROM the school, the trees seemed to stretch out bigger above us, and the drying leaves of the oaks crackled as the crisp September breeze played among their branches. An evergreen branch snapped back in my face, grazing my cheek, and I got a whiff of lemons and Christmas trees. I squatted down to push my hand into the deep green cushion of moss covering the softened outline of a stump. I let the others walk just a tiny bit ahead. I took a deep breath in and let it slowly whistle out.

Finn led us to a small clearing. We all stood around, shifting from foot to foot and jumping up and down to stay warm. "It's chilly," Anna Perkins said to no one in particular.

Cat pulled off her Duke Basketball beanie and handed it to Anna. Anna pulled it down over her ears, and Cat pulled up her sweatshirt hood and tugged on the strings so only her eyes and nose were visible. We were going into uncharted territory: to a place where someone like Anna Perkins borrowed clothes from someone like Catherine Fisher. Anything was possible.

The sky was white overhead, as though the clouds were fifty feet away instead of thousands. I was hoping Finn had a plan, something to keep us out there and away from the stale-smelling cafeteria. Finn cleared his throat. He was wearing a red-and-black checked vest over his khakis and polo, which made him look like a cross between a lumberjack and the garden gnome Mom's sister, Sheila, brought us from her trip to Norway. "The game is called Sardines," he announced, like he was reading from a list of scheduled events. "Someone hides, and everyone else has to find that person, and when you do, you hide with them. The goal is not to be the last one searching. Got it?" When we all nodded, he said, "Okay, I'll go first."

We closed our eyes and listened as the sound of Finn's footsteps grew softer and softer. Cat counted to one hundred. When she stopped, I opened my eyes, blinking at the sudden brightness of the sky. We looked at each other and began to walk in the general direction we thought Finn had gone. It wasn't good to stay all together; then the point of the game would be lost. Robbie gave a whoop and took off running ahead. I veered back toward the parking lot, thinking I would walk along the edge of the woods in case Finn was hiding in one of the bigger trees with long, low branches. Anna and Cat went the opposite way, and soon all I could hear were the leaves crunching under my feet and my breath, slightly ragged from the fast pace I was walking. Usually I avoided running, since I hated the sound of my breath heaving and the pounding feeling in my chest. But something about being in the woods made me feel lighter, invincible.

I carefully checked in the branches of each tree, looking for shoes or the bright color of some clothing. I was so busy looking up that I almost didn't see the large boulder with an L.L.Bean boot sticking out to one side. When I peered over the top, Finn and Cat were grinning up at me. I smiled back and sank down in the leaves beside them, trying to move as slowly and noiselessly as possible. The ground was cold but dry. With my head against the large stone I listened to the soft sounds of the others' breathing. Then, suddenly, Anna was there, sliding in beside me!

The fake fur around the collar of her pink puffy coat

tickled my neck. She smelled good, like laundry detergent, and not the kind Dad and I used from the machine at the Laundromat that burned my nose a little bit if I sniffed it. But even better than the way she smelled was how she turned and smiled at me as we sat there waiting for Robbie to find us behind the rock.

When Robbie finally stumbled upon us, we all cheered. "Who found you first?" he asked.

"Catherine did," Finn said.

"It's Cat," she said.

"Cat Fisher?" he asked. "Like the fisher cat? *Martes pennanti* of the northern boreal forest?"

She shrugged. "Uh, I guess."

"Fierce creature," Finn said.

Cat sprinted off while we stayed to close our eyes and count. This time Anna found her first. When it was my turn to be it, I lay down next to a huge deadfall pine tree and covered my legs with leaves and pine needles. I was alone in the woods, but it was a different kind of alone, different from the emptiness of our house without Mom in it. The woods were full of small noises; it was peaceful, even if I was all by myself. Robbie was the first to find me, and then Finn, who hopped gracefully over the log and lay down like he had known we were there all along. Robbie took a deep breath in. "Fall's awesome," he whispered. "How come we never did this before?"

"Andrea," I said.

"Oh yeah, she had like a focaccia about bugs."

I looked at him quizzically.

"Uh, what's that called when you're really scared of something?"

"Phobia," Finn said.

"Yeah, that," Robbie replied.

"Shh," I said, so we wouldn't get found. But then, before either Cat or Anna could get there, we heard Steve holler into the woods, calling us back to the cafeteria. Parents were starting to arrive.

Robbie's mom was first. She usually was. Robbie had two younger brothers and a sister. I sometimes saw them gumming up the windows of his mom's minivan. Robbie's mom always got out of the car to come get him and usually greeted him by kissing the top of his head, something that was possible because Robbie was still so short and because, I guessed, despite turning bright red whenever she did it, he kind of liked it. When he got into the van, always in front as the oldest, I got the feeling he was going somewhere warm, filled with the smells of whatever was cooking for dinner.

The next to arrive was Anna's mom. Her sleek black

BMW rolled to the curb, where it sat puffing an almost invisible line of exhaust into the sky. Anna got up wordlessly and shouldered her purple backpack. She looked resigned, but then turned back to the table where Finn, Cat, and I were sitting and gave us a little half smile and a wave before she left.

Cat's mom was next. She had glittery pink lipstick and shiny red nails like talons. It was hard to look at Cat and imagine that the two were related. Still, she gave Cat a short side hug before pulling her hoodie off her head as they walked out together.

And then it was just me and Finn. No matter how late Dad got there, I always left before Finn. Whatever his parents looked like, they were a mystery. I pictured them a lot like him—weird, old-fashioned, like from another time. I imagined they were college professors or artists, jobs where you didn't come home covered with tiny white flecks of insulation dust like my dad did.

We sat across the table from each other. I wanted to hold on to the feeling from the woods, but instead I stared out the window behind Finn's head, wondering how cold it would get that night and if my comforter, which I'd had since I was five and which was losing more feathers every day, would be enough to keep me warm. I didn't want to ask

Dad about the propane tank, which I was pretty sure was sitting empty on the back of the house. Mom always took care of those things, or at least she used to before Charlie died. In the last year it seemed like we got more bills in urgent red envelopes. They piled up on the coffee table and in the junk drawer next to the sink—it was something Mom and Dad fought about when they thought I was sleeping.

Finn had his baseball pen out and was twiddling it between his fingers again. "I saw a good place," he said. "A hiding place for tomorrow." I nodded vigorously. Sardines was something to look forward to. When my dad finally rolled up in the truck, I hopped up from my seat and zipped my sweatshirt up as high as it would go. I tried to think of a cool way to say goodbye but I couldn't come up with anything, so I just gave a wave, kind of like Anna had, and said, "Bye."

Finn smiled. "Goodbye, Lucas."

When I got home, I slid out of the truck and walked behind our trailer to an area called the Pine Grove. The Pine Grove was the one thing Charlie really liked about where we lived. He could really remember the different apartments we'd lived in, and even the one golden year when we'd rented a whole house. Charlie hated living in the Box—that's what he called our single-wide. He'd say,

"Let's get out of the Box," or ask me, "Why do you want to hang around the Box?" if I'd been home all day. He could say stuff like that, even around Dad.

Most of the trailer homes at Oak Hill—you leave off the *Trailer Park* part if you live there—were empty in the winter. A bunch of retired people showed up from Florida around May and stayed for the summer. The old people were nice enough. I think they really enjoyed having kids around. They always gave me snacks and asked how I was doing. The Pine Grove was their place. They had potluck cookouts there, and on Sundays a few of them even had a little church service. Charlie and I liked to go back there and make little gnome homes out of the rocks, sticks, and pine needles that collected there. Sometimes we would even bring my Lego guys out and set up a whole city and have battles and stuff. Now the Pine Grove was where I went when I wanted to think about Charlie and be by myself.

The sun was sinking behind the trees. I plunked myself down on the ground, leaning back against one of the stumps the summer people used to make a campfire circle, and began to brush the pine needles together with my hand. The ground beneath them was soft and spongy but not damp. I imagined a pine-needle hut big enough to stand up or sleep in—safe, warm, and dry, and away from everything. If I closed my eyes, I could pretend Charlie was there, pushing up mounds of pine needles with his hands or lying on the ground and carefully arranging little rocks into a garden path or sticks to make a roof for the hut. When the breeze blew, I could almost feel his hand ruffle my hair and rest on my shoulder. I felt warm on the inside. I stayed out in the Grove until Dad yelled for me to come in.

CHAPTER 6

"WHERE'S FINN?" ROBBIE SAID.

I scanned the cafeteria, and it occurred to me that I had never once seen Finn at lunch.

"You mean that weird kid who wears church pants?" Peter Kapinsky asked. "He's in the library"—he paused—"reading the newspaper."

Both Robbie and I chewed on this alongside our lunch. I knew kids who didn't like the cafeteria, but I didn't know any kids who willingly read the newspaper.

By October we had fully explored the woods behind the school and knew most of the boundaries. On one side there was the teacher parking lot and the cafeteria. On the far side you ran into the backyards of the people who lived on Blackstrap Road, and running along one edge you ended up by Memorial Park and the town ice rink, currently just a big open field and an empty wooden warming hut. The last side was the most interesting. It didn't really have a boundary that we could see but sloped downward until the ground got really swampy and the trees draped with light green moss.

"What is that?" Anna asked.

"Probably an old hunting blind," said Robbie, still panting from our third round of Sardines that afternoon. We were all staring up at the wooden platform fifteen feet off the ground, the rungs of a ladder nailed into the tree below it.

The old hunting blind was halfway up a tree at the edge of the swamp, and the ground around us was squishy with bright green moss.

Finn slowly circled the tree, his face excited in a way I hadn't seen before. Then, just as quickly, the excitement turned to drama. "That is the future of this enterprise," he said solemnly. "Let us consecrate this holy moment with a ritual. Nothing will ever be the same." He reached down and scraped a fingerful of mud from the ground and used it to paint horizontal lines across the top of each cheek. A few dry oak leaves stuck out from his hair, making him look like an elf king.

I was holding my breath, waiting for one of us to laugh but hoping that no one would. I didn't know what *consecrate* meant, but I wanted it to mean something good and important. Anna gave a nervous giggle.

"I can almost smell it," Finn said.

We all sniffed deeply. "Skunk?" said Robbie.

"Something is happening here. The winds of change are blowing." Then he reached over and painted a stripe on Robbie's forehead. I thought Robbie would bat his hand away, but he didn't. And he didn't stop Finn when he crushed some dried leaves in his hand and sprinkled them over his head.

"Me too," said Anna, and she stepped forward to be decorated by Finn, and then Cat did too. At last Finn stood in front of me and smeared a cold muddy finger down my nose and across my cheeks. I tried not to look at him, afraid I might crack up and mess up the moment. But Finn's eyes seemed to be looking at me and through me at the same time.

"Let us ascend," Finn said. I held my breath as he grabbed each rung and pulled himself up and then onto the platform, out of view. "Come on up," he called. "She's old but sturdy!" One by one we followed him up. I waited to go last, figuring that if I fell, at least I wouldn't take out Anna on my way down. But the boards were easy to grip even with the worn-out toes of my old sneakers, and the branches after that were spaced closely together with wide, easy footholds.

Since I was the last one up, I found a spot on a branch a little bit apart from the main platform, afraid the whole thing might creak or even break if I put my full weight on it. "This is excellent," Finn said, patting the boards on either side of him. "Really quite sturdy, all things considered." He peered down at the base of the tree. "There are a few more boards down there. With the right tools this could really be something."

"Like what?" Anna asked.

"A refuge," Finn said. "A retreat."

We all got quiet for a minute. I thought of Charlie and the Pine Grove and wondered why Finn needed a place to retreat.

"Lucas," Finn said, "does your dad have any tools?"

"Yeah, some." Dad and Charlie had done Pinewood Derby every year for Scouts. Every year they built a car and raced it. Really, Dad built the car and tried to get Charlie to help him, but Charlie wasn't that into it. Charlie and Dad always fought when they tried to do stuff like that together, because Charlie wanted to jump around and skip steps and

Dad had this really long way of explaining everything and wouldn't let him touch the tools until he was done talking.

I couldn't wait until it was my turn to make a car. I had the design all planned out in my head. But the year I was finally old enough, Dad's hours changed at work and he couldn't come to any of the meetings. I made the car on my own to surprise him. When I finally unveiled it, he asked me suspiciously, "Who helped you with this?" I thought he would be proud that I'd done it all myself. But instead he barely patted me on the head and muttered something about how no one really needed him anymore.

I thought about his carpentry tools buried in the back of the closet. Barely even touched since I quit Scouts the year before. Dad would never let me bring his tools to school. But it might be worse if I borrowed his stuff without asking. "There's some that he hasn't used in forever. He probably wouldn't notice if I borrowed them for a day or two," I told Finn.

"Greatness comes to those who balance risk and reward in equal measure," Finn said.

"Is that a quote or something?" Cat asked. "Who said that?"

"I did," Finn replied.

"I could try," I offered.

Finn just nodded like he knew I was going to anyway.

Steve smirked at our painted faces when we marched back in at the end of outside time. Louise made us wash up in the bathroom, but for the rest of the evening I got a little whiff of the woods every time I shook my head or touched a hand to my face.

That night, while Dad snored, shaking the thin paperboard doors and walls of the Box, I snuck out of bed to the closet at the end of the hall where he kept his carpentry tools. The dented black metal toolbox was covered with dust and creaked when it opened, but inside I found a hammer, a bunch of odd wrenches and screwdrivers, a measuring tape, and a level. I took the hammer and grabbed a small handful of nails from each of three cardboard boxes, figuring Dad would be less likely to notice if I took a few of each kind. I shoved it all in a gallon ziplock and wrapped the whole thing in my gym shorts before sliding it into my backpack. For once I was glad to have a parent who never checked my bag for homework or school notices.

CHAPTER 7

HAVING ALL THAT STUFF IN MY BACKPACK MADE ME
nervous. I didn't know if there was a rule about bringing
tools to school, but I wasn't about to ask anybody. As soon
as I got to my locker, I pulled out the hammer and nails
and shoved them way down in the bottom. Robbie was
watching me and gave me a big thumbs-up. Greg Hutchins
must have been watching too, because he walked by us on
the way into homeroom, made a face, and gave a really obvious thumbs-up to Robbie. Then he and one of his friends
started cracking up. Robbie's face got all red and blotchy.

"Hey, Robbie," Greg said, "I like your backpack." Then
he gave him another thumbs-up. Robbie's backpack had a
big Minecraft sword on it; maybe it was a little babyish for

middle school, but why did Greg care? The whole thing made me wish I were brave enough to stand up for Robbie, or quick enough to think of something smart to say back. Or, at the very least, small enough to crawl into my locker and pull the door shut behind me.

In math class we had a substitute, which meant worksheets that probably no one was ever going to look at. The sub was an older guy with a gray ponytail who wrote his name, Mr. Romero, in cursive on the board and probably just wanted someone to pay him to read the paper, because after he handed out the worksheets, he did exactly that. Sadie Gillespie tried to ask him a math question, but apparently he didn't give a very good answer, because she just rolled her eyes and sat back down, looking frustrated. I did a few of the problems, enough to look like I'd made an attempt, and then doodled in the margins and watched the clock, waiting for the period to be over.

Suddenly Cat, who sat a couple of rows ahead of me, spun around and glared at the two girls sitting behind her, who burst into giggles. That was enough to disrupt Mr. Romero's newspaper reading, because he lowered the paper and told everyone to settle down, which of course did nothing. A minute later Cat whipped around again and nearly shot fire out of her eyes. This time me and half the class were watching to see what would happen next. The two girls waited a minute, and then one of them leaned forward cautiously and yanked at something near Cat's head. Was it hair? Were they pulling her hair? This time Cat didn't turn around; instead the two girls collapsed over their desks, snorting and laughing into their arms. I heard one of them say something about a horse tail.

Cat got up and walked to the front of the room to grab the bathroom pass. Then as she walked back down the row toward the door, she pushed hard on the girls' table so that their books and pencil cases went clattering down onto the floor.

"Girls!" Mr. Romero called out. "Clean up that mess!" But Cat was already at the door, and the two of them got stuck picking up everything themselves. I was holding my breath, waiting to see if she would get away with it. When I turned around to look at Finn, he had that look again, like when we found the tree fort. His hands were pressed together and his fingers were tapping gently in a repeating pattern.

That afternoon, Ms. Edgerly started a new unit on atoms by reading us a picture book about a little animal called a pygmy shrew. She made us sit on the rug instead of at our desks, and she showed us each page like we were in kindergarten. Some kids grumbled about being treated like babies, but being read to was a lot better than doing worksheets or listening to a lecture. The book was about how everything gets smaller and smaller until you get to atoms. And even then things get smaller: bits of atoms called protons and neutrons. And she said what was even weirder was that if an atom were the size of a house, the nucleus would be only the size of a grain of sand. So that meant that these tiny things that made up everything in the universe were mostly just empty space.

At that point a lot of kids were playing with their shoelaces or flicking carpet lint at each other, but not me. I totally got that: sometimes my insides felt just like that atom. Ms. Edgerly looked right at me, and even though I had written her off after that first day, I stared back at her and nodded because I wanted her to know that I got it. She looked like she was going to smile at me, but it was more like a sad smile, and then she sent us all back to our seats.

As I walked down to Teen Club at the end of the day, the hammer and nails tucked into my backpack thudded against my back. I heard footsteps behind me and suddenly the weight was lifted. Cat was holding the backpack up by the loop in the back. "Is that what I think it is?" she asked.

"Yeah, I got a few things."

"Cool," she said, and when she smiled, her whole face was transformed. "That's the only reason I came to school today."

I wanted to tell her that I'd seen what the girls did in math or that I thought her response was pretty impressive. But then why didn't I say anything or do anything about it at the time? We were at Teen Club before I could sort these ideas out in my head.

Steve barely even looked up from his phone when I grabbed my backpack before heading outside. Finn was carrying his bag too. Instead of a backpack, like the rest of us had, he carried a small maroon duffel to school. Once we were under the tree, Finn put his bag, which was bulging in a funny way, to the side. I shook the hammer and nails out of my backpack into the leaves. Finn squinted at the materials. "I suppose Lucas should go up there and the rest of you can hand up the boards."

"I'm not sure," I started to say.

"I'll come up too," Finn said. "I've got an idea about how this could work." Then he winked. "I'm the vision; you're the labor."

I climbed up first, taking each step carefully so I wouldn't slip, willing myself to be light enough to climb without the boards creaking and groaning beneath me. Finn scampered up after me and perched near the edge, carefully examining each board that Cat, Robbie, and Anna handed up. If he couldn't identify its original location, he found a new spot for it. I used more nails than we probably needed: three on the end of each board.

"Bravo!" Finn said at one point when I nailed a board in a particularly tricky spot. Finn had me reinforce the boards that made up the floor, and then we added a couple more to create a perch so someone could sit a little bit above the main platform. Finally, we nailed some large pine boughs in place so the whole thing was more difficult to spot from below. It took us two full outdoor rec periods to finish. At the end of the second afternoon everyone climbed up to see what we'd accomplished. That's when Finn opened his bulging maroon duffel and pulled out an old glass jar like the kind people made pickles or jam in.

"There's one for each of you," he said, reaching into the bag again and again like Santa Claus until there were four identical jars in front of him.

"For what?" Cat asked.

"For a wish," he said. I glanced around, but everyone looked as confused as I was. He reached into his pocket, pulled out an acorn cap, and dropped it into one of the jars, which he pushed toward me. "For a job well done."

"Uh, thanks," I said.

Finn held another jar up. "Fill your jar with acorn caps and your wish will be granted."

Cat squinted at him. "Like magic?"

"Whatever it takes," he said. "Sometimes you have to ask the universe for what you want."

There was a long pause. I stared at the jar, my jar, the one with a single acorn cap inside like the nucleus at the center of the atom. If I stared at it long enough, would it transform into a black hole that could suck me back in time to before Charlie died and Mom left? That seemed like a lot to put on an acorn cap.

Robbie had a blank look on his face—like how he looked whenever he was called on in class, waiting for the teacher to move on. Cat was cracking her knuckles and looking past Finn at something in the woods. What if no one played along? Suddenly I wanted that wish—I wanted to believe it was possible to ask for something and get it.

"Okay," said a voice. "I'm in."

CHAPTER 8

ANNA REACHED ACROSS THE CIRCLE AND GRABBED HER
jar. She took a sparkly pink hair elastic from her wrist and
pulled it around the rim of the jar. "So I know it's mine,"
she said. Cat shrugged and grabbed a jar. I took one for
Robbie and pushed it toward him. Robbie held the glass
up to the light as if he were looking for cracks.

"What about you?" he asked Finn.

"I prefer to referee," Finn said cryptically.

"So how's this work?" Cat asked. "What's the strategy?
What are the rules?"

"You can only find acorn caps in the woods and only
during afternoon rec. When your jar is full, we'll convene
and decide how to grant your wish." Finn recited this the

same way he had explained the rules for Sardines.

"What if someone cheats?" Robbie asked.

"Are any of you planning to cheat?"

We all shook our heads.

"Okay, then," Finn said. "Let the games begin."

For the next week we burst out the door after snack time and split up into the woods, kicking over the leaves and twigs, searching for acorn caps. By the end of the second day we knew where every oak in the woods was located. We pushed over logs and peered in every hollow in every decaying tree. No one said anything specific about their wish, but we all searched the ground like hawks hunting our prey. I tried to imagine what the others might want: a new game system or a trip to Disney? I couldn't imagine telling them what I wanted. It all seemed impossible, but if anyone else had doubts, they didn't say anything.

When I got a couple of caps in my pocket I kept one hand on them, rubbing their textured surface with my fingers as my eyes scanned the ground. It was so calm and so quiet in the woods. I could hear my breath in slow, even puffs and the occasional crack of a tree bending in the wind. Sometimes I would cross paths with Cat or Anna or Robbie. Sometimes we would even walk together, squinting at the ground with equal intensity.

When I walked by myself, I thought about Mom and sometimes Charlie. It wasn't always sad—it was nice in a weird way. Most of the time I kept my memories of Charlie locked away because I was afraid of the power they might have: I didn't want to burst out crying in the middle of the cafeteria or in gym class or something. But out in the woods there was air to breathe and space to move. And while I walked around, kicking over sticks and piles of leaves, I also kicked things around in the secret corners of my mind.

"Kid," Charlie said, "I've hit the jackpot."

My arms were too short to reach into the thicket and get the fattest berries where they hung just below a blanket of prickly branches and fuzzy leaves. The blackberries ripened in the middle of August, when it was still hot but the nights turned cool, when fall and school were right around the corner. They were dark and plump and bursting with juice. I could place one in my mouth and barely even chew. Just a little pressure and the whole thing would explode with sweetness on my tongue.

"No way," I said. "This is the jackpot right here." I was

squatting on the ground, turning over branches overlooked by birds.

"You don't know what you're talking about, kid," Charlie said.

I snorted in response and popped another berry in my mouth. The Tupperware that Mom had given us to fill sat empty on a tree stump behind us. Eating them right off the bush was perfect when they were warm and even tasted like the sun.

"I've got to go to practice, kid," Charlie said. But he didn't budge from his spot deep in the thicket.

After a few more minutes had passed, I said, "Coach will bench you if you're late."

We looked at each other and grinned. No one benched Charlie, even when he was late. And it wasn't because he was an all-star probably going to UMaine on a full ride. Everyone just loved Charlie. Even when they tried to be angry at him, it didn't work.

I smiled, thinking about him as I walked around the woods outside school. When I had four or five caps in my pocket, I would make a trip to the tree fort, climb up, and deposit my loot. Finn was there. He stayed in the fort, usually reading an old book with a dark blue cover and faded gold lettering: *Great Expectations* by Charles Dickens. Sometimes I heard him harrumphing or laughing to himself, so I figured it must be good. At first I was a little annoyed, annoyed that his life was so good he couldn't even come up with anything to wish for. But maybe that wasn't it. Maybe he just played by an entirely different set of rules, or a different game altogether.

Whatever it was, I knew I was a long way from understanding what made Finn Clark work. Each day that we were out there, he brought something new for the fort in that old maroon duffel of his. First it was a fuzzy Winnie-the-Pooh blanket, then a thermos, which he sometimes convinced one of the cafeteria ladies to fill with hot water for tea. There was an old tackle box with a rusty lid, which he filled with tea bags and little packages of soup crackers. Some stuff he never even used; he just seemed to like making the place homey.

Soon there was a problem: I had more acorn caps than anyone else, and I was not ready to share my wish. I shook the jars and then sat there for a bit, watching Finn read and wondering if I could just go back down without putting what I had in the jar. Finn spoke up from behind his book: "Nothing says you have to put them in your own jar."

"Okay," I said quietly. I dropped one in my own and one

in each of the others. After that, I made sure no one else followed me when I climbed up to the fort, and I always placed my acorn caps evenly in the other three jars, adding just enough to my own to avoid suspicion.

It was the end of October and it was starting to get cold in the woods. We all wore our winter coats, except for Finn, who added a blue-and-white wool sweater to his lumberjack-meets-garden-gnome outfit. It was nearly time to go in when Cat dropped the final caps into her jar to fill it. Finn blew on his hands and then held Cat's jar aloft. "So what's your wish?" he said.

I was sort of surprised. I guess I had expected something more ceremonial. Or somehow I'd thought Finn would already know, the way he knew I wanted to play the game but didn't want to win.

We all looked at Cat. She set her chin and said, "I want to cut my hair."

We were quiet for a minute.

"So," Anna said, "cut it."

Cat shook her head. "My mom won't let me." She pulled the long brown ponytail, which she always wore at the nape of her neck, around in front. "I hate my hair," she said. "But my mom said it's bad enough I dress like a boy; she's not going to let me cut it." Her voice dropped. "She said if I ever did, she'd take away basketball."

"If you cut your hair, she won't let you play basketball?" Anna sounded surprised. "That's mean."

"What if you waited until after basketball season?" Robbie suggested.

"We could cut it for you here," Anna said excitedly.

"That's not a solution," Finn said. "That's defiant rebellion."

"So?" Anna said.

"So it wouldn't really solve the problem," Robbie spoke up. "And if we did it, they'd find out about this place and they would take it away." He was quiet for a moment. "Before anyone else got their wish."

His face was anxious. It was not the look of someone who was going to lose an Xbox or even a shot at Disney. Maybe Mom was right about people's insides and outsides. "We'll think about it over the weekend and reconvene on Monday," Finn said. Just then Steve's voice called out in the distance that outdoor time was up. It was getting darker earlier, and our time outside was shrinking day by day.

CHAPTER 9

"I'VE GOT TO WORK TOMORROW," DAD SAID AT DINNER
that night.

I was trying to saw through the congealed mass on
my plate, spaghetti doused with a can of tomato sauce
and powdered with sprinkle cheese. I wasn't complaining,
though. Dad usually made an effort on Friday nights. He
could cook three things: spaghetti, scrambled eggs, and
steak. Steak was expensive, so we never had it anyway,
and scrambled eggs stuck to the pan, which I would end
up washing, so spaghetti, even if it was one big lump, was
really the best option.

I sucked up a single noodle, smacking myself in the
side of the face with sauce as I did.

Dad shot me a look of disgust. "Do ya have to eat like that?"

"Sorry." My appetite disappeared. I pushed the noodles and sauce around on my plate, wondering what had made my mother love him in the first place, if she ever did.

Dad is a jerk. Dad is a jerk. I repeated it over and over again in my head. Sometimes I substituted a worse word for *jerk*. Thinking it made me feel mad instead of sad, and mad was easier. Dad should know; he was the king of mad over sad.

I knew the story of how my parents met: in chemistry class in high school. They were assigned to be lab partners. Mom set her hair on fire, and Dad put it out with the fire blanket. Maybe that was supposed to be romantic, but to me it seemed a little lacking when you were thinking about spending your life with someone.

"Your father is an honorable person," Mom said. What did that even mean? I wished she were here so I could ask her. "His father wasn't a good role model," she told me when Dad was being especially jerky. This didn't make me feel any better and even made me worry more about what kind of person I could expect to grow up to be.

When she wasn't super tired from working a long shift at the diner, Mom wrote poems and stories. She made up whole worlds with dragons and wizards and people with incredible secret powers. Sometimes she told them—or what she called the "kid version" of them—to me at bedtime. But I don't think she ever shared them with Dad. When he saw her sitting there with her notebook and pencil, he would say something like "Cat got your tongue?" or "Everything right where you left it?" A stupid question that didn't mean anything except that he didn't understand what she was doing or why she was doing it.

Dad finished everything on his plate, just like always, and gave a look of disapproval to my leftover spaghetti. I expected that he would get up, grab another beer from the fridge, and then plant himself in front of the TV for the night, but instead he pushed back slightly from the table and pulled a folded-up sheet of blue paper from his back pocket.

"Why didn't you tell me about these parent conferences?" he said, unfolding the blue flyer that must have come in the mail.

"They're not for a while," I said.

Dad looked at the flyer again. Then, after a long pause, he said, "Mom usually goes to these." It was kind of a question and kind of not. It was also the first time he'd brought her up in weeks.

"You don't have to go," I said quickly. "As long as you

check my grades on PowerSchool at least once."

"Your teacher called me. She asked if I was coming in. Said she was a little worried about you. You seem sad. You don't talk much."

"They always say that in conferences. I never talk much."

Dad nodded. "Yeah, that's what I figured. I used to get that too. 'Needs to participate more.'"

Wait a minute. Was he trying to relate to me? "Mrs. Lynch, she's your teacher?"

"For homeroom and English."

"You tell her anything about this? About us?"

About Mom, I thought. That's all he cares about. He doesn't want to be embarrassed in front of my teacher. He doesn't want to think anyone is feeling bad for me, because that would be like someone is feeling bad for him. I scowled. "No."

That seemed to satisfy him. He got up from the table and went to the fridge, looking for a minute as though there were actual choices to be made. "That PowerSchool thing. You need a computer for that?"

"No, you can use your phone."

"Huh." Dad pulled his phone out of his pocket and tapped in his pass code. Then he slid it across the table to me. "Think you can set that up?"

I started to swipe over to the app store to download the PowerSchool app to his phone, but as I did, his most recent notifications popped up. There were several missed calls from two different area codes outside Maine, and a bunch of texts from Mom's sister, Aunt Sheila. Dad had his head in one of the kitchen cabinets checking on his side hobby: catching mice. I could hear him talking to himself as he repositioned his glue traps. My heart was pounding in my throat as I grabbed a pen from the center of the table and scribbled down one of the numbers.

Dad whipped around and squinted in my direction. "What are you doing?"

I looked him right in the eye. "Creating a password for you," I lied.

"Jesus, not another password. Keep it simple, all right?"

"Sure," I said, hoping I looked cooler than I felt. "I can set it up so it will be saved in your phone and you won't have to enter it every time." As quickly as possible, I downloaded the app to his phone and put in the login Mrs. Lynch had given me. I changed the password to Bruins37—37 for Patrice Bergeron, Dad's favorite hockey player—and then nudged his phone back across the table to him. He glanced down at it briefly.

"How are your grades?"

"Okay," I said.

"Okay."

"Is Mom in Massachusetts?" I asked.

Dad stared down at his phone as if PowerSchool could tell him how I knew to ask that. "What makes you think that?"

"I don't know. You said she was at a hospital."

"It's a treatment program."

"Okay, well, I don't know why we can't visit her. So I guess I just figured she had to be somewhere far away. Aunt Sheila lives in Massachusetts."

Dad scowled. He and Aunt Sheila did not get along, and that was putting it extremely mildly. "Yeah, well, she knew about a program there. She's always butting in where she doesn't belong, playing the big sister."

I felt a surge of warmth. I knew where Mom was! And then, just as suddenly, my heart sank. Massachusetts was far, and the part where Aunt Sheila lived was even farther. And what if this meant Mom was moving there for good?

"I still don't understand why she can't call."

"She'll call when she's ready," Dad snapped. He got up from the table and walked out the front door. I could hear the doors of the truck opening and slamming, like he was looking for something. Mad over sad every time.

I dumped the rest of my food in the trash and put my plate in the sink, while I ran water for the dishes to soak. Then I went and lay on my bed and flipped an acorn cap back and forth between my fingers. My room was small, but I had a window that looked out into the woods. Dad grew up in the woods, on twenty acres of old farmland. His parents sold it when they moved to Florida. He used to drive us by it and talk about saving up to buy it back. Then the new owners turned it into a housing development, and Dad stopped driving by or even taking the road that went past it.

On the shelves above my bed there was a full set of the hardback Harry Potter books along with the Lightning Thief and Wings of Fire series. The next shelf held my best Lego creations. I had a few sets—I'd gotten them for Christmas and my birthday over the years—but the main source material was under my bed: two huge boxes of Dad's old space Legos. I pulled one out and began to mindlessly snap the pieces together, thinking about Mom.

All this time I had assumed she couldn't call because they wouldn't let her. Whoever *they* were. But Dad had made it sound like Mom had a choice, like she could call if she wanted to. The thought of that made me sick. What kind of program was this, anyway? The sour taste of tomato sauce crept back up my throat, so I tried to think of a solution for Cat instead. It was a better problem to think about than any of the ones closer to home.

CHAPTER 10

MRS. LYNCH WAS UP AT THE BOARD, DRAWING A PLOT diagram for the book *Tangerine*, when something flicked me right in the face and I heard a whispered, "Oops." It was the tiniest note I'd ever seen, smaller than my pinkie fingernail. When I unfolded it, the words *I got it!* jumped out in bright green bubble letters.

When I looked up, Anna caught my eye. She mouthed the word *sorry* just as Mrs. Lynch turned back from the board. "Anna, can you tell us about the rising action?" Anna's eyes got wide as she stared blankly at the board.

"I don't know," she said quietly.

"Well, let's make sure we're listening, then," Mrs. Lynch said brightly.

When we were done plotting the diagram, or diagramming the plot, Mrs. Lynch gave us time for independent reading. I hadn't really picked anything, so I went over to Mrs. Lynch's shelf and stared at the choices.

Suddenly Anna Perkins slid up next to me. "I figured it out! About Cat," she whispered excitedly. "I think I figured it out."

"It's reading time, not chatting time, Lucas and Anna," Mrs. Lynch called from behind her desk.

Anna's friend Lauren Dinardo, one of the popular girls, snickered. I glanced over my shoulder in time to see her give Anna a look that seemed to say how ridiculous it was that Mrs. Lynch thought that *we* were chatting. I couldn't see Anna's face to know if she was embarrassed or not, but she quickly walked back to her seat.

I pulled out the fourth Harry Potter book and went back to my desk. Mom and I had read them all together a long time ago, but when I reread them, I remembered her favorite parts—anything with Hagrid or Professor McGonagall—the parts that made her sad, and the characters she couldn't stand, like Dolores Umbridge.

Mrs. Lynch stood over me and gave a friendly sigh when she saw my book selection. "Have you read that before, Lucas?"

"Yeah."

"I thought we talked about you challenging yourself a little bit?" I looked over her shoulder at the kids in the beanbag corner, who were holding up their books and using their phones behind them. "You're a very strong reader," she said. I pictured myself with huge biceps hefting encyclopedias over my head. "That's why I want you to push yourself and find some more challenging books to read."

"You said rereading was okay."

"Yes, that's true. But I want to make sure you're going outside your comfort zone some of the time." She gave me a big, forced smile. "That's our job as teachers!"

I heard a little snort-cough behind me and looked over my shoulder. Cat was suddenly pretending to be very interested in her biography of Sheryl Swoopes.

"Okay," I said. I stared through Mrs. Lynch's head at the bulletin board just behind her. There was a picture of her with her husband and kids on a boat somewhere. They looked really happy, and something about it made my stomach burn. I wanted to tell her, *Every day when I go home, I'm out of my comfort zone!* Well, I didn't want to tell *her* exactly, but someone. I thought there should be someone overseeing this whole thing. Someone who would say, *Hey, that kid's not in such a great situation.* But whoever that person was, they hadn't shown up yet. I knew Mrs. Lynch was waiting to hear me say I would change my book or read something harder next time, but I wasn't going to do it. I waited until another kid came up to her with a question and picked up my book again. Harry was going to enter the Triwizard Tournament and eventually he was going to win. The rising action, the falling action, all of it would lead to that moment. I already knew how it was going to turn out; no matter what happened at home or at school, nothing could change that.

In gym class we were doing a basketball unit. There were a bunch of stations set up around the gym, and we were supposed to rotate through all of them. I was practicing dribbling around a set of cones when I caught sight of Cat at the other end of the gym, sinking free throws. Cat was impressive when it came to free throws. She bounced the ball twice, aimed, and fired, nearly always hitting her target. But that wasn't what grabbed my attention. Under the basket, leaning against the blue gym mats, were Greg Hutchins and Kyle Moriarty. They weren't even in our gym class, but there they were, and every time Cat went to shoot, they would wave their arms or yell "air ball" or something stupid, trying to mess her up. I looked around the gym, but our gym teacher, Mrs. Cannistraro, was down at the other end helping some kids learn to set a pick.

Finally, Greg and Kyle headed for the door, but before they got all the way out, Cat took the ball and hurled it sidearm at their backs. I sucked in so hard I thought I might have pulled all the room's air into my lungs. The ball bounced off the back of Greg's head and ricocheted over to the bleachers. Cat jogged after it, her head down but a smile on her lips. Greg's yells finally got Mrs. Cannistraro's attention, and she shouted at them to get back to class. I just stood there, wide-eyed and open-mouthed, wondering what it would feel like to do something with all the anger I felt boiling inside of me instead of just swallowing it back all the time.

When we finally went outside at Teen Club, it felt really good to walk into the woods. The cold air went shooting up my nose and straight down into my chest, cooling the burning feeling that had lodged itself there during English class. We went straight to the fort; Anna was practically skipping, she was so excited. I wondered if she'd had a chance to tell anyone else her idea for Cat, and for a second I was jealous of Robbie, who had every class with Anna.

"Hey, Lucas," Robbie said as we marched and crunched our way through the underbrush. "Are you going out tomorrow night?"

"Huh?"

"For Halloween," he said, and then added nervously, "I have to take my brothers and sister out, but I figured I'd throw on a mask and get some candy too."

Dad would think I was too old to trick-or-treat. Mom would have let me go. I looked over, realizing suddenly that Robbie was waiting for an answer.

"I don't know," I said. "Probably not."

"Oh, okay," he said. "Well, if you change your mind, our neighborhood is really good. Some people even give out regular-sized candy bars. You could come over and go with us if you want. My brothers and sister are pretty annoying, but you get candy.

"You don't have to decide right now. You can let me know later if you want," he added.

It had been a long time since anyone had invited me over. I used to go to birthday parties—you know, when it was an unwritten rule to invite the whole class—but then the invitations stopped coming. I just assumed nobody thought of me as having out-of-school-friend potential. Maybe I was wrong. Robbie seemed genuinely disappointed that I couldn't go. I felt bad for letting him down, so I said, "Where do you live?" Not that it would matter, but at least it would give me a decent excuse.

He smiled wide, so I could see he had a little piece of apple stuck in his braces. "Right near you! I mean, you live in Oak Hill, right?"

He was nice enough to leave off the *Trailer Park* part. I nodded.

"We live on Libby Lane. It's right through the woods. I could even come and walk you over if you want." My stomach dropped. "I mean, if your parents say it's okay."

"Okay, maybe."

"I'll give you my number."

"Hurry up, you guys!" Anna shouted back at us. "I can't wait to tell you my idea!" She had already scaled the ladder into the fort. She was leaning out, little wisps of hair flying away from her face and her eyes shining.

Up in the tree fort our breath came in little white puffs. Finn sat cross-legged, while I leaned back against a branch, waiting to hear Anna's plan. She waited until we were all staring at her expectantly.

"Locks of Love," she said.

"Huh?" said Cat.

"I saw it at the mall. I was in Hair Excitement with my mom and I saw a sign for it. It's a thing where you get a free haircut if you donate all your hair to make wigs for people with cancer. You need to have at least ten inches of hair, but you totally have that."

"Yeah," Cat said slowly. "But my mom isn't going to care that the haircut is free. She just doesn't want me to cut my hair."

Anna deflated. "But don't you think she'd let you if you told her it was for a good cause, like people with cancer?"

"Maybe," Cat said. But we could all tell the answer was no.

"We need a new perspective," Finn said. He spun around so his back was toward us, then lay down so his head was in the center of the circle and propped his legs up on a tree branch. "Come on, try it."

One by one we all lay down on the wooden planks that made up the fort and turned our heads toward the cold white sky, our view bisected by evergreen branches. "Isn't that better?" Finn asked. It was better. Even though the wooden boards were cold against my spine, I felt flat and even and level: held to Earth by the same gravity that everyone else was. Ms. Edgerly had told us that no matter the mass of an object, gravity would pull it to earth at the same rate of acceleration. And just as I was thinking of anything but Cat's hair, an idea occurred to me.

"What about parent-teacher conferences?"

"What about them?" Cat said.

I took a deep breath. "Well, we have to do that goal-setting thing. You know, an academic goal and a personal goal. And maybe your personal goal could be to help people. You know, people with cancer."

"Lucas, that's an amazing idea!" Anna said. I was glad we were all lying down so no one could see me blushing. "Mrs. Lynch would go crazy about that. She always makes such a big deal out of having specific steps. Your steps would be getting your hair cut and donating to Locks of Love. And your mom will be at conferences, right?"

"I guess so," said Cat. But this time there was a tinge of hope in her voice.

"I think she even has to sign off on your goals!" Anna was bursting. "Oh my God, this is totally going to work, you guys! There's no way your mom is going to deny you in front of your teacher and everything." She got quiet and sat up, reaching across the circle for her own jar of acorn caps, which was more than half full. She shook it thoughtfully and said, "This could really work."

CHAPTER 11

MY BEST HALLOWEEN COSTUME WAS THE YEAR I DRESSED up like a Minion. Charlie and I were obsessed with the *Despicable Me* movies. We had all of them on DVD and watched them so many times that even Dad could do a passable Gru accent. For Halloween, I wore overalls and painted my face yellow, and I made an eyeball out of a camping headlamp. Charlie went as Gru. He was fifteen—and probably way too old for trick-or-treating—but he took me out and even dressed up in a suit with a long fake nose. I came up with the idea to make the nose out of Silly Putty. Charlie said it was awesome. He said it was his best costume ever. And I could tell he really meant it. We went all over the neighborhoods near our apartment, and he never seemed embarrassed to be out with his little brother. He didn't seem to care what other people thought.

Halloween was a crazy day at middle school. Teachers made kind of a pathetic attempt to channel the energy by having a school spirit day with the grades divided by decades. Sixth graders were supposed to be the sixties, seventh graders the seventies, and eighth graders the eighties, but most kids just wore whatever weird stuff they wanted. Anna and all her friends wore matching tie-dye shirts. Greg Hutchins and his friends all sculpted their hair into multicolored Mohawks. I didn't really think that was sixties, but I wasn't going to say anything. Finn came to school wearing a weird white wig and carrying a paintbrush and a Campbell's Soup can.

"What are you supposed to be, homeless?" Greg Hutchins asked him. A couple of kids laughed.

"Nope," Finn said. "Guess again!"

"Oh, Finn!" said Mrs. Lynch when she interrupted math class to ask Miss LeGage a question. "You're Andy Warhol! The famous painter," she added, surveying our confused faces.

Finn beamed and Miss LeGage smiled nervously. I bet she didn't even know who Andy Warhol was. Everyone had candy, and some teachers just showed movies, I guess so we would sit and be quiet. Sadie Gillespie, who had to know everything about everybody, said that Greg and his friends had to go to the principal's office because they brought fake switchblades as part of their costumes. How dumb could you be?

Maybe it was all the candy making me crazy, but when I got home that night, I dared to ask Dad about going over to Robbie's to trick-or-treat. To take his brothers and sister trick-or-treating was actually how I phrased it. If Dad was going to say no, at least I wouldn't give him the chance to make me feel like a baby for wanting to go out on Halloween.

"I'm not driving you anywhere tonight," Dad said.

"You wouldn't have to," I said quietly. "He's just on the other side of the woods."

Dad grunted. It wasn't a yes, but it wasn't a no.

I used the home phone to call Robbie, and I think he was really surprised to hear from me. I was almost out the door with my pillowcase and my *Friday the 13th* mask when Dad jerked up from his place on the couch. "Where are you going?" he said.

"You said I could go to Robbie's."

Dad squinted and said, "Don't be too late."

I wanted to say something smart—like *Oh really, you're*

going to be a parent now? You won't get off your lazy butt and drive me to my friend's house, you didn't get any candy for Halloween, and you didn't even ask me for the number where I'm going to be. Really great parenting, Dad. But I didn't say any of that. I just shook my head and purposefully let the door slam behind me because I knew he hated it.

I knocked on Robbie's door and it was like I'd entered Narnia. Robbie's mom immediately asked me if I'd had dinner and if I wanted any of the pizza they were just finishing up. I thanked her but said no, I'd already eaten, which was true if you counted ramen noodles as dinner. She put her hand on my shoulder when she asked, and I felt a hollow place open up just below my ribs.

"Actually," I said, "I am still a little hungry."

"Of course you are," Robbie's mom said. "You're a growing boy!" She told me to call her Jeannie, but I was too nervous to do that. I slid into a seat at the kitchen counter island, where Robbie was wolfing down a slice of pepperoni. There were three other plastic plates scattered around the counter with bits of crust and cheese left on them. "Sorry it's such a mess around here. The little ones are really excited to go out trick-or-treating. Are you sure you two can handle taking them?"

Robbie rolled his eyes. "Mom, I already told you. We'll be fine."

"Do you have brothers and sisters, Lucas?"

"Um," I said.

"Mom!" Robbie blurted out.

"It's okay," I said. "I had an older brother, but he died about a year and a half ago." It would be two years this Christmas, but I held on to those half years because it meant less time and space between me and Charlie.

"Oh, sweetie, of course. I'm so sorry. Robbie told me all about it and I just went running my mouth off like an idiot." Her face was flushed, and I felt bad that my life was making her feel bad.

"This is really good pizza," I said, taking a huge bite so I wouldn't have to talk for a bit.

"You think so?" she said brightly. "It's the kids' favorite. But I think it's a little greasy. I like Amato's better." There was a loud crash from upstairs, and Robbie's mom looked up nervously. "I'd better check on them," she said.

When Robbie's mom left the kitchen, I looked around at the many art projects and framed school photos that lined the wall. In addition to the ones of the four Belcher kids there was a photo of a boy wearing a school uniform who didn't quite match the rest of the family. Robbie had pale pinkish skin that threatened to sunburn in mid-March. This boy had an olive skin tone, and deep brown eyes. He was missing his right front tooth in the photo. "Who's that?" I asked.

"That's Pascal," Robbie said. He pointed at a jar on the counter stuffed with change and a few dollar bills. "Mom adopted him through one of those Save the Children programs. She always wanted more kids, but after the twins, my dad was like, 'No way!' She calls Pascal her fifth baby. You should see the letters he writes her." He rolled his eyes. "She's saving money so we can go visit him someday."

Robbie's mom reappeared, pushing her hair out of her face. There was a smear of orange glitter on one cheek. "Well, you're in for some fun tonight," she said. "I told the kiddos that if there's any funny business, you're to bring them right home. And make sure they say thank you." There was a loud clatter as three pairs of feet came thundering down the stairs. Mrs. Belcher grabbed them at the bottom of the stairs and handed out flashlights. "This is Marcus—he's a Teenage Mutant Ninja Turtle. Alex is a vampire. Julia's the zombie Barbie doll."

"I'm not a zombie Barbie, Mommy. I'm a Monster High doll. It's a totally different thing." Mrs. Belcher looked at me and shrugged her shoulders. The look she gave me was nice, like I was one of the grown-ups too.

"Listen up, you three," she said. "Robbie and Lucas are in charge of you, so don't do anything bad or they'll bring you right back here and there'll be no more candy."

They were halfway out the door before she even finished talking.

"They don't seem that bad," I said to Robbie as we jogged to catch up to his siblings.

"Two words for you," Robbie said. "Evil genius."

As soon as we were past the Belchers' front lawn, Marcus swiveled around and shone his flashlight directly in my eyes. "We're not going five ways on this. Robbie, if you want to share your twenty-five percent with him, that's up to you."

"Fine, whatever," Robbie said.

"What was that all about?" I asked as we practically sprinted to keep up.

"Evil genius. Marcus is the mastermind, but they split all their candy equally at the end of the night. They're bonkers about it."

Marcus, Alex, and Julia set out at a fast pace, with Marcus in the lead. They bypassed the first two houses and turned up the sidewalk at a well-lit house with two big trucks parked in the driveway. A tall blond woman came to the door, and when she opened up the screen, Marcus said, "Boo!"

The woman cackled with delight. "Honey, it's the Belcher kids," she called to someone behind her. "Aren't they cute. Here, kids, take a couple."

She loaded up each of our bags with several candy bars before she sent us on our way. Marcus skipped the house next door in favor of the one after that.

"What about that one?" I asked as we passed by a perfectly acceptable-looking house with fake cobwebs in the trees and pumpkin lights in the windows. Marcus took a device out of his pocket and swiped before studying it. He ignored my question and walked up to the door at the next house. Here he paused before ringing the doorbell and looked at Julia. "You're up," he said.

When the owner of the house came to the door, the boys crowded Julia out. She pushed her way through and said in the tiniest little voice, "May I have some too, please?"

The man at the door just about fell over himself trying to make sure that Julia got plenty of candy, since her brothers were clearly not letting her get her share. At the next house Alex brought out a cardboard collection box that said Pennies for Peace on it. That earned all three of them a serious load of candy in addition to whatever pocket change the woman at the door was able to fish out of her purse. Something was definitely up. "Is that a real charity?" I asked Robbie.

He shrugged. "I told you, evil genius."

Julia might have been the smallest, but she was by far the best actress. She had a routine that involved crying and saying she had dropped all her candy in the dark. Flashlights were put away for that one. And another routine had her rubbing her knee and asking for a Band-Aid before relieving the unsuspecting do-gooder of half their candy bowl. At the end of their street we turned right and then left without discussion, clearly following a preplanned route.

"We have to be back in about twenty minutes," Robbie warned them at a little after eight o'clock. Marcus stopped and took out his device again. It looked like an older iPhone. He jabbed at it for a minute and then turned around to take a side street we had just gone past.

"What, is he using GPS or something?" I joked.

"Worse," Robbie said. "He designed his own app. It uses public records, like people's land value, home prices, how old they are, and stuff, to figure out the best houses to stop at. No senior citizens handing out single plastic-wrapped butterscotch candies or boxes of raisins."

"What? Seriously? Where did he find that?"

"He didn't find it. He designed it. Like he wrote the code and everything. I told you: evil genius."

"Do your parents know?"

"Yeah, at first they were kind of freaked out. But now there's a company that wants to buy it from him, and they might pay him a lot of money for it. So I guess they're pretending it's cool."

We followed Marcus, Julia, and Alex up the steps of a very large brick house with white columns on either side of the front porch. Robbie hung back a little and I stood next to him, not wanting to interfere in whatever the evil genius had planned for this house. Robbie pushed his Spider-Man mask back on to the top of his head. "You know whose house this is, right?"

"Nope."

"Look in the driveway."

Coming up the front walk, we had passed right by the shiny black BMW. With the bright security lights shining down, I could easily read the plate. It said *BANKR*. My stomach jumped up my throat. I swallowed hard.

"She's probably not home," Robbie said.

I nodded. Anna Perkins was probably off doing whatever

the popular kids did on Halloween. But then she opened the door.

"Trick or treat!" Alex, Marcus, and Julia chimed. They were all wearing Care Bears masks—I hadn't even seen them make the switch.

"Oh my God," Anna said. "You guys are so cute!" She held the bowl down low so they could pick their treats. Then she looked past the trio to where Robbie and I were standing. She smiled at us and then glanced nervously behind her. "Hey, Robbie. Hey, Lucas." She held up the bowl of candy. "You guys want some?"

"Who are you talking to?" a voice came from inside the house. It was a kid's voice, a familiar voice. "When is your mom coming back so we can stop answering the door and finish the movie?"

I glanced over at Robbie, who had gone pale at the sound of the voice.

Anna looked embarrassed and pulled the door closer to her back as she extended the candy bowl toward us. What should we do? Was it lamer to take the candy, or pretend like we weren't there for candy? Just as Robbie reached into the bowl, the door was yanked open and we were looking at Greg Hutchins, Nicole Watson, Lauren Dinardo, and a whole group of the popular kids from Feltzer Harding Middle.

Robbie's hand shot back, crumpling the Reese's peanut butter cup in his hand like he had been caught stealing.

"No way!" Greg Hutchins said. "You guys out trick-or-treating?"

Anna rolled her eyes. "So what, Greg? You just said like half an hour ago that we should all put on costumes and go get some candy."

Greg snorted. "Whatever." Then he called back over his shoulder. "Hey guys, look who it is. It's Robbie—" And then he swallowed a big gulp of air and let out a huge burp. I could almost smell the Dorito cheese from across the porch. The other kids, except for Anna, all laughed like they'd never heard someone burp before. But when they stopped, one person was still laughing: a loud, barking fake laugh. It was Marcus.

"Wow, dude," Marcus said, his voice dripping with sarcasm, "that was brilliant. How'd you ever come up with that one? Because our name is Belcher, right? You lose a few brain cells over that one or what?"

One of the kids behind Greg Hutchins started to snicker and said, "Dude, you just got roasted by a kindergartener."

"I'm in third grade, smart guy, but I'm sure a kindergarten

kid could have taken this moron down just as easily."

Now all of the popular crew was laughing. Marcus flipped his Care Bear mask back down over his face and said, "Peace. I'm out." This only got everyone laughing harder, except for Greg Hutchins, who looked furious, and Anna, who looked embarrassed and uncomfortable. Robbie and I followed his brothers and sister off the porch and out of the yard without saying goodbye to Anna. I thought it was pretty awesome that Marcus had managed to make one of the cool kids at Feltzer Harding look like a complete loser, but Robbie looked pale and worried.

"Evil genius?" I suggested, hoping to make him feel better.

Robbie just shook his head. "Hutchins is going to destroy me for that."

"He'll forget about it," I said, even though we both knew that was unlikely.

CHAPTER 12

Dear Lucas,

I'm so sorry to leave without saying goodbye. I thought it would be easier this way. As soon as I have some things figured out I will send for you. I'm sure you think I'm being selfish. You're probably right. I love you more than you can know.

Mom

The day Mom left had actually been a pretty good day. I was helping Mr. Boudreau clean out one of the trailers they rented by the week during the summer. Inside one of the kitchen cabinets I found a glass jar filled with quarters, and he said I could keep it, plus he gave me ten bucks for helping him. I saved the ten bucks and took a bunch of the quarters to the game room at Wasamski Springs—the town swimming area just a couple of miles away from Oak Hill. I played a bunch of Ms. Pac-Man and some of the other old-school games they had there, went for a swim, and even treated myself to a freeze pop from the snack bar. I was walking back along Route 77, enjoying the feel of my damp towel slapping against my legs, when Dad pulled up in his truck. I knew something was off because it wasn't even five o'clock and he wasn't wearing his work clothes.

I got into the truck but he didn't pull out onto the road. Instead he put the truck in park and pushed his hands back through his hair, knocking off his dusty Bruins cap. "Mom had to leave. She's gone."

"What do you mean, 'gone'?"

Dad pushed his hand back through his hair again, stretching his face so for an instant he looked just a little bit older than Charlie. "I don't know what to tell you exactly. Mom needs help. You know?"

I shook my head.

"She's sad all the time. She doesn't get out of bed. She . . ." He faltered.

"She's not sad *all* the time," I said. "And she's tired a lot because she works a lot. On her feet, all the time."

A switch flicked and Dad's voice got that all-business

tone he used when he was asking me to do something for the second or third time. "She's leaving, Lucas. She's going to be away for a while. That's all I know."

"Is she going to say goodbye to me?" I felt my voice trembling, threatening to break.

Dad started the truck up again, but it was already running, so the engine squawked in protest. Dad swore. "Jesus! I don't know, Lucas!" He sounded mad. At me or Mom or the truck, I didn't know. When we got home, I ran inside and through each of the small connected rooms as if she might be hiding somewhere. But she wasn't. She was gone and so were her things. The tiny blue and green glass jars she collected were missing from the windowsill. Her books had left rectangular dust-free prints on the shelves, where only a few of Dad's tool catalogs remained. There were several empty spots on the fridge where she had pulled off the few family photographs we had printed from when Charlie was alive. We hadn't taken one since. Now maybe we never would.

For some reason I looked in Charlie's old room, but it was still just filled with piles of things Mom and Dad had brought home from his dorm room and old stuff from high school that he'd never bothered to clean out.

That first postcard came a few days later. I crumpled it

up and threw it on the floor after reading it, but the details were burned into my memory. She would send for me. That made things okay for the first couple of weeks, made it seem less permanent. But it was November now. The longer it went, the more incredible it seemed. My parents had had fights, but I thought all parents had fights. They never threw things or hit each other. More than anything their fights were quiet: they barely spoke to each other, and when they did, their voices were tight and tired and angry. What if something had happened to her? Maybe I would never know. Maybe nothing had happened to her and she had just decided to walk away from me and Dad forever. Maybe I was stuck with this churning acid feeling under my ribs for the rest of my life.

The morning after Halloween, Dad left early for work. Next to a Rite Aid flyer on the kitchen table was another postcard, folded in half like it had been in his pocket for a while. I was afraid to look. What if she had found another family, some other kids to be a mother to, and this was her final goodbye? Anything seemed possible. I ate my cereal slowly, knowing that whatever was on that card might make it impossible for me to swallow another mouthful. When I was done, I rinsed my bowl and put it in the drying rack.

I looked at the clock. Twenty minutes until the bus came. I picked up the card again and looked at the image on the front. There was a picture of a pond with some ducks, and cattails lining the sides. Somewhere called Look Park. Stupid name for a park. I could already see that there wasn't much written on the card. Finally, I took a deep breath and read.

Dear Lucas,

I'm so sorry I haven't been able to call. Even writing this postcard is hard. I'm working hard to be the person you need me to be, and when I'm better I will send $ to Dad so you can come and visit me.
Love,
Mom

Visit her? My face burned. Who did she think I was? Didn't this place have a phone? We still had a home phone. And even though I'd used it yesterday, I went over and picked it up, just to make sure Dad had kept up on at least one of the bills. What would it be like to hear her voice? I was so mad, so boiling mad, I couldn't even imagine talking to her. I thought I would just scream and hang up.

That's how I was when the bus pulled up at the entrance to Oak Hill. I couldn't even smile and say good morning to Mr. Paul, who always had a smile for every kid who got on his bus. I stalked straight to the back and slid into a seat, staring out the window but seeing nothing the whole way to school.

I was still simmering during the class geography bee when my social studies teacher, Mr. Bennett, asked me to name the country whose capital was Bucharest. That's why I said, "I don't care!" And I walked myself out of the room and down to the principal's office before he could send me there himself.

That's how I ended up sitting outside the office next to Finn Clark.

Finn got there after I did, and he had a real pink slip in his hand.

"Lucas!" he said, as if this were a pleasant coincidence. He winked and said, "We'll be derelict criminals together, then! True desperadoes!"

A smile twitched around my lips in spite of everything. It was hard to stay mad about anything when Finn was, well, being Finn. He sat down next to me and started humming. I didn't know what to say to that, so we sat there for a while without saying anything. Finally, my curiosity got the better of me, and I tried to peek at the pink detention slip folded over in his hand. He unfolded the paper and held it out so I could read. There was only one word, written in block letters and punctuated with a large exclamation point. *INSUBORDINATION!*

"What does that mean?"

"According to the *OED*, it's 'refusal to obey orders, defiance of authority.' I suppose it's because I refused to participate in the school geography bee."

"Me too," I said. Just then Mr. Coughlin, the assistant principal, came out of his office and saw us sitting on the bench. He had a sandwich in one hand and did not look like he'd expected anyone to be there. He sighed and took a large bite, which caused a glop of mayonnaise to plop onto his tie. He swore not quite under his breath, so Finn and I looked immediately in the other direction and pretended we hadn't heard.

Mr. Coughlin dabbed at his tie and beckoned us both into his office with his sandwich hand. The assistant principal's office was surprisingly unimpressive—just some framed certificates on the wall and a shelf of books with uncracked spines and titles like *Reading Is for Everyone*.

Mr. Coughlin looked expectantly at us once we were sitting across from him. "So," he said after the moment stretched a bit too long, "why are you boys here?"

"We refused to take part in the school geography bee," Finn told him.

Mr. Coughlin looked exasperated. "Whatever for? Did you plan this together? This better not be another one of those student protests against climate change or some other nonsense."

We shook our heads.

"Mrs. McCafferty told me I had to at least try, and I told her it wouldn't be fair to others," Finn said.

"Why ever not?"

"Because I've memorized the world atlas."

Both Mr. Coughlin and I looked disbelievingly at Finn.

"An outdated one, for sure, but nonetheless still accurate about most things post–Soviet Union and whatnot."

Mr. Coughlin turned to look at me. "Have you *also* memorized the world atlas?"

"No," I said, shaking my head. "I just didn't feel like it."

Mr. Coughlin took a minute to rearrange the pens on his desk. Then he picked up a bunch of papers, lined them up at the edges, and set them back down again. He seemed kind of stumped. "Well, boys, I think you know better. We all need to try our best, isn't that true?"

Finn and I both nodded.

"You need to at least try," he said directly to me. And then, turning to Finn, he added, "And if you win, well, then it's not as though you cheated. Frankly, you might have a real shot at the state bee. It would be nice to see Feltzer Harding in the news for something besides contaminated lunch meat." Then he wrote us each a pass to go back to class.

On the way out of the office we passed Ms. Edgerly standing at the photocopier. I expected her to scowl again, but instead she raised her eyebrows at me, and I could have sworn she winked before turning back to the copy machine.

CHAPTER 13

"FINN IS GOING TO WIN THE GEOGRAPHY BEE," I TOLD everyone at the fort that afternoon. We were lying with our heads in the center staring up at the blank sky. Robbie was on one side of me and Cat was on the other.

"I'm sorry I was rude to you guys last night," Anna said suddenly. If I twisted my head backward I could see her striped leggings and the soft brown fur of the slipper boots that all her friends wore.

"It's okay," Robbie said.

"No, it's not," Anna said. "You guys are more my friends than most of those people who were at my house. I don't even know why some of them were there. Half the time I think they're saying things about me behind my back."

"So why are you friends with them?" Cat asked.

"I don't know," Anna said. "It's like they all came together in some kind of weird deal. Nicole's mom works with my mom at the bank, so she was really nice to me when I first moved here. I was so freaked out about being a new kid and not having any friends. She acted like she really wanted me to be friends with her and her friends. It felt weird to get a whole group of friends together like that. But it was better than having no friends. And now I'm afraid that if I don't hang out with them"—she paused and took a deep breath—"then I won't have any friends at all. Anyway," she said, "I'm sorry Greg was such a jerk."

"He was a jerk way before you ever moved here," Robbie said.

"Thanks," Anna said softly.

"My sister says it's better when you get to high school," Cat said. "She reads a lot of books about the future, like *The Hunger Games* and *Divergent*. She said middle school is kind of like that—like all postapocalyptic and stuff with people trying to figure out their factions and where they belong. It's like they think the only way they can do that is by making other people feel like crap. But Tessa said in high school people are still in groups and whatever, but they're not such jerks about it. Like the theater kids have their group and the sports kids have their group, but they're not so mean to each other."

Mom said it only took one. She always said that you only really needed one good friend to get through things. She still talked about her best friend from high school, even though Dad got kind of annoyed about it. His name was Asher Rhinegold. Mom said he was really smart. He won the state science fair by creating some kind of robotic thing that helped people with disabilities walk better. Every year we got a Christmas card from his family in Seattle, Washington. She talked about Asher, and I knew she used to be friends with the woman who owned the supermarket in town, but she never really mentioned anybody else. Mom was super nice and everyone seemed to like her, but maybe she was lonely too. It was weird to think about your parents that way.

It made me think of Harry Potter and the Sorting Hat. At least at Hogwarts everyone got to be in a House. The hat never sorted anyone into a loser or leftover house. Where did I fit in? I didn't play sports, and even the thought of getting up onstage in front of a bunch of people made me queasy. There had to be a place for kids who didn't quite fit anywhere else, didn't there?

CHAPTER 14

THE ENTIRE SCHOOL WAS CRAMMED INTO THE GYM FOR the geography bee finals. All of us sixth graders were twitching on the floor, trying to avoid that awful feeling when parts of your butt fall asleep. Meanwhile the seventh graders loomed over us in the bleachers, and the eighth graders were up around us on the second-floor elevated track. They leaned over the railing like the audience at a gladiator's bout. They were huge, and some of them even had facial hair! My hand went up to my own soft, hairless cheek. It seemed as likely as turning into a butterfly or a sprouting a pig's nose.

Most of the kids in the geography bee went out after one round, getting everything wrong from the capital of France (not London) to the name of the Continental Divide (the Rocky Mountains, not the Mississippi River). Finn sailed through all the early rounds with ease, never hesitating on an answer, until finally he was one of the last two standing. His competitor was a tall eighth-grade girl named Abigail Reese. She had a shiny brown ponytail and small squinty eyes and seemed a little bit annoyed to be sharing her stage with a sixth-grade boy who barely made it up to her shoulder. To make matters worse, the crowd was all cheering for Finn.

There was a burst of applause and shouts as Finn got another answer right. Anna turned around and gave me a huge smile. I smiled awkwardly back and then looked away so I wouldn't start blushing. Everyone had been cheering for Finn the loudest since he'd corrected Mr. Flanagan, the school librarian, on the pronunciation of Djibouti. Djibouti, pronounced "Juh-booty," was apparently a small country in Africa. Mr. Flanagan tried to say it like "Dee-sha-booty," which would have been funny enough as it was. But then once Finn corrected him and got the reaction from the crowd, he kept it going by giving the population and the percent of arable land and highlighting its Lac Assal, the third saltiest body of water in the world. The eighth-grade boys went crazy. They couldn't get enough of Finn and started chanting "JA-BOOTY" over and over again as loud as they could. Meanwhile, Abigail Reese just rolled her eyes and tossed her ponytail.

Mr. Flanagan was an older man with a few hairs combed over his otherwise bald head and a seemingly endless collection of reading- and library-related T-shirts. He sat in the middle of the gym at a table with Mrs. Kelley, the school secretary, who was probably just thrilled to be out of the office for the day. The two of them tried to get control of the crowd again, but by that point total silence was pretty much impossible.

In order for someone to win the whole thing, the other person had to get a question wrong *and* then the winner had to follow up with a right answer. The questions ping-ponged back and forth for a while, and the eighth-grade boys were getting louder and wilder every time Finn got one right. Abigail Reese must have memorized an atlas too, because she knew a lot about geography. But where she seemed nervous and flustered by the competition, Finn looked totally calm. He never seemed to be thinking that hard about the question. He just opened up his mouth and right answers kept popping out.

Assistant Principal Coughlin came in after a while,

looking really excited. I bet he was thinking about whoever won going to the state bee and maybe removing the rancid-lunch-meat stain from the Feltzer Harding Middle School reputation. There was a guy with him with a big camera, and he was pointing at Finn and Abigail and tapping notes into his phone. It figured that the school geography bee was going to be big news in the *Springfield Ledger*.

But when the guy with the camera showed up, Finn started looking nervous. He was jiggling his leg and squinting at the doorway where the newspaper guy and Mr. Coughlin were talking. After another round or two our guidance counselor, Mrs. Verzoni, went up to the table and whispered something in Mrs. Kelley's ear, who in turn whispered something in Mr. Flanagan's ear. Of course, we all got quiet then. Now they were both looking at Finn. Mr. Flanagan coughed and said, "Uh, due to the deadlock we find ourselves in, if neither contestant can win in the next round, then we'll have to have a written exam. Whoever gets the best score goes to the state bee." Everyone cheered because that meant it was almost over.

Abigail answered a relatively easy question about the location of the Vatican, and then Finn got one about the mountains that separated Europe and Asia. "The Urals,"

I whispered. It seemed likely that this contest was going to end without a winner. But then Finn got a funny look on his face.

"Djibouti," he said. "The Djibouti Mountains."

There was a moment of silence before the gym erupted in laughter and thunderous applause. The eighth graders started chanting Finn's name. Finn looked strangely pleased with himself. Mr. Flanagan waved his arms around to get the crowd to settle, and when that didn't work, he yelled into the microphone until there was a screech of feedback, which only made everyone scream and grab their ears. Finally, a very flustered Mr. Flanagan looked sternly at Finn and said, "I'm going to have to accept that as your answer."

"I know," Finn said. "I just guessed."

I looked up at him, incredulous. How could he not know the answer? *I* knew the answer. Probably half the sixth grade knew the answer. It had been a question on our landforms quiz two weeks before.

Abigail Reese was declared the winner to polite applause and seemed to get suddenly very fond of Finn, patting him on the back and shaking his hand. But I felt cheated. I think every sixth grader in the gym felt a little cheated. We filed out of the gym and back to class, our butts numb, our legs aching, and our pride wounded.

When I asked him about the final question later that afternoon in the woods, he gave a very Finn-like answer. "It seemed like it meant more to her than it did to me." But he wouldn't meet my eyes when he said it. I couldn't help but wonder if it had had something to do with the sudden appearance of the newspaper reporter.

When Dad picked me up that evening, he was in a good mood. I could tell because Tom Petty was on the radio and he was singing along. I looked for other clues, other things out of the ordinary, but there wasn't anything really obvious. He was wearing his work clothes, his hands were creased and dirty as usual, and his lunch cooler was empty at my feet on the passenger side. The only thing unusual was his phone, which he usually kept buried in his pocket, out on the seat next to him. He kept tapping it and glancing down and smiling really weirdly.

When we pulled into Oak Hill, he drove past our trailer and parked the truck near the Pine Grove. "Come on," Dad said, opening the truck door. "I want to show you something."

All I wanted to do was collapse on the couch, but instead I followed him back through the Pine Grove toward the woods and the path that took me to Robbie's neighborhood. But then Dad veered off the path in a different direction.

I picked my way through the underbrush, trying to think up a homework-related excuse that would end this weird adventure. Before I could come up with anything, he stopped in front of a little shed. It was no more than six feet across and maybe a little more than that deep, but unlike some of the ice-fishing shacks that collected weeds in other people's yards, someone had taken the time to shingle this one and put a real glass pane in the window. Instead of sitting on concrete blocks or a trailer, it had four stone corners, almost like a real foundation. And there was something that looked like a skinny chimney poking out of the top.

Dad took a key out of his shirt pocket and unlocked the padlock holding the door. He pushed the door open and I peeked inside. There was a tiny woodstove, a desk, and a chair, and not much else. Dad looked behind me into the woods as he spoke. "I thought your mother might want somewhere to write. You know, her stories and stuff. I didn't get a chance to show her." He coughed. "Anyway, I thought maybe you could make some shelves, use it for your Lego stuff, maybe invite your friend over and use it like a clubhouse or something." He looked at me.

I couldn't have been more surprised if Dad had shown me a closet full of spy gear and fancy tuxedos. "Yeah, sure," I managed to sputter out.

He put the key in my palm, and just for a second I could feel the warmth of his calloused fingers. He turned and walked back toward our trailer without saying another word. I pushed the door to the ice shed open and took a step inside. The small wooden desk had a top that could flip open. I ran my finger down the well-worn pencil groove.

I tried to picture Mom in the space. I could see why Dad had thought she would like it. I imagined her sitting with her feet propped up on the table, pointing them toward the woodstove, her hands wrapped around a mug of hot tea. It was the nicest thing he had ever done for her, that I could remember. But she was gone.

CHAPTER 15

I THOUGHT ABOUT WHAT DAD SAID ABOUT ASKING ROBBIE
over to show him the clubhouse or maybe just dig around for
stuff in the woods. But whenever I started to say something
the words seemed to get stuck in my throat. What would
he ask about Mom, or the fact that there wasn't much food
or much of anything? I told myself I could wait to ask him
over until after Dad went to the store or maybe once Mom
was back. Besides, Robbie wasn't like me—he had other
friends he probably invited over all the time.

At the end of science class one day Greg and Kyle and
a couple of other guys circled around Robbie's desk.

"Merry Christmas," they started saying to each other,
even though Christmas was still more than six weeks away.

"Merry Christmas." They kept saying it and then cracking up when the other person said it back. Then they looked right at Robbie, and Greg said, "Hey, man, Merry Christmas. Say 'Merry Christmas'!"

My throat and my mouth went dry as a desert, as if I were the one in the center of their circle. I tried to lick my lips but they felt like cracked cement. Robbie shrugged. "Merry Christmas," he said quietly.

"It's not Christmas—what, are you an idiot?" Greg said. And then he cracked up so hard. Like saying Merry Christmas in November was the dumbest thing you could ever think of. And Robbie just sat there, his face turning bright red, trying to pretend like he was in on the joke instead of the joke itself.

The next day Cat came to school late. She walked into English class with her hood pulled tight around her face. When she sat down in her seat, she turned around and looked right at me and Anna before she shook the hood down onto her shoulders. Her long mane of brown hair had been chopped just below her ears. Anna let out a little squeal and I gave her a really dorky thumbs-up that I hoped no one else saw. Then Mrs. Lynch coughed loudly, so we had to go back to our silent reading. When we got out to the fort that afternoon, Cat was still grinning, and her face almost looked like it was glowing. I wasn't sure if it was the short hair or just how good it seemed to make her feel, but either way the warmth was catching.

"How does it feel?" Anna asked her.

Cat touched the edges of her short hair poking out from underneath her hat. "Cool. Like me. It feels like me."

Finn didn't say much, but he was humming a little song under his breath and smiling.

Some afternoons we played Sardines, round after round until Steve yelled our names into the darkening afternoon sky. It was practically dark by four thirty, and the twilight gave the game a new excitement and intensity.

The colder weather meant that the little swampy puddles near the fort froze over with thin sheets of ice that made a satisfying cracking noise when we stomped on them. Back behind the fort we found the remnants of an old dump. There was some newer stuff on top—couch cushions and cardboard beer boxes—but underneath were some cool old glass bottles and weird twisted-up pieces of metal. Robbie was really excited about looking up the old bottles online to see if they were worth anything.

The fort started getting crowded with our collections: bent spoons and forks, a picture frame without any glass, some oil cans, and these tightly coiled springs that must have come out of an old couch or chair. We joked about hitting the jackpot—finding some amazingly rare old thing that we would sell for lots of money and split five ways.

"What would you do with the money?" Anna asked.

Robbie said he would get a really fast sports car—a Ferrari or maybe a Porsche.

"I want a full-sized basketball court at my house," Cat said.

"I would move back to Hawaii," Anna said.

"That's where you lived before?" Cat asked. "And now you live here? Wow, that must make it really suck."

"I guess, but even worse, in two more years we'll live somewhere else. The Coast Guard makes us move every four years. But if I had all that money, we could move back to Hawaii and never move again. Sometimes when I think about it, it's just like a dream I had. Like how could a place like that ever really exist?"

"It is really like in the movies?" Robbie asked. "Like palm trees and monkeys everywhere?"

"Coconuts," I said quietly. Everyone turned to look at me, and then they started laughing. I didn't realize I'd said something funny.

"Lucas," Anna said, "you're so random." But she meant it like random-funny, not random-weird.

"Yeah," Cat said. "'Coconuts.' Like it's all quiet and then, just, 'Coconuts.'"

The giggles died down and then Robbie asked me, "Is that what you'd buy? Coconuts?"

"Yeah," I said, "mountains and mountains of coconuts." Everyone busted up again, and I thought maybe I'd be off the hook for answering.

But Anna looked at me seriously and said, "No, really. I want to know what you would do with the bazillion dollars we're going to get from whatever we find out here."

"Okay," I said, staring down at my shoe and tugging on the place where the sole was starting to separate from the rest of the sneaker. "I'd buy my mom a castle in England or somewhere like that where they have castles. A real castle." I didn't look up in case they thought I was incredibly lame.

"Awww. I think that's really sweet," Anna said. It was quiet for a minute, and I picked furiously at my shoe, not wanting to meet anyone's eyes. I didn't add that I would live there too, that all I could think about sometimes was getting away from my dad and the Box. I didn't say it because even though it was mostly true, I was starting to realize that if I left, I would miss the four of them. I wasn't sure what to do with that information or dare to think that they might feel the same way about me.

"What about you, Finn?" I asked without looking up.

Finn looked slowly around at the fort and all of us. "I'd buy this."

"A tree?" Robbie said.

"A little cabin, a place that was all my own. Quiet and warm."

"Around here, or in Djibouti?" Robbie said, and we all cracked up.

"What about your family?" I asked.

"Oh, they could come too," Finn agreed. But something about the way he described it made me picture him on his own. Finn held up each of our acorn-cap jars and shook them a little to settle the contents. It was either going to be Anna or Robbie next; both jars were close to full.

I stalled a little when everyone went down the ladder to look for acorn caps or sift through the junk pit. Then it was just me and Finn, and I thought of something I'd been wanting to ask him.

"How do you do that?"

"Do what?"

"Memorize an atlas."

"Oh, something to pass the time when you haven't many friends." I hadn't expected this answer, not at all. "I like to imagine all the places in the world: long stretches of beach with only a few little fishing shacks; mountaintops with stone huts and thatched roofs; vast cities filled with old stone buildings, tiny little gargoyles on each corner, attic apartments crammed full of books and historical artifacts." His eyes glowed as he described each of these distant places. I couldn't help noticing that Finn's imaginings had no people in them, and even though they sounded exciting, they also sounded kind of lonely.

"Additionally," Finn said, "I think I may have a photographic memory. I study a page and then it's just all there. All I have to do is recall the page and I can see it, just like I'm looking at your face right now."

"That's cool," I said.

"Sometimes."

"Well, I mean, you probably don't even have to study in school."

"Nope, not really. But the thing is, I can't really control what I remember and what I forget." He sighed and then gave me a look that was serious and a little sad, like a very old man recalling his childhood. "Aren't there some things you'd rather not remember?"

When I got home that night, I went to the bookshelf next to the TV and picked up one of the few framed photos Mom had left behind. It was a picture of Dad with two-year-old Charlie on his lap. They were on a friend's boat. Charlie looked a little annoyed, his pudgy face squished by the padding of his life jacket. Dad was staring out at the water, his hands firmly around Charlie's body and his lips just brushing the top of Charlie's head.

Dad walked over to see what I was looking at. I thought he was going to get all annoyed and say something about dwelling on the past. Instead he took the photo from my hands and stared at it, letting out a big sigh before he set it down again.

CHAPTER 16

THE MORGUE WASN'T A SAD PLACE. IT WAS A COLD place with no feelings at all. The waiting room had a bulletin board with nothing on it but a typed paper saying you had to ask if you wanted to post anything there. There was a table in the corner with a fake plant, a few flyers from the middle of the newspaper, and one empty paper cup. Mom and Dad took turns going in to see Charlie while I sat on a plastic chair, staring at that paper cup. I wasn't thinking about Charlie. I wasn't thinking about anything. When Mom came out, she wrapped her arms around me, pressed her face into the top of my head, and cried into my hair. When Dad came out, he asked me if I wanted to see him.

"You don't have to," Mom said quickly.

Dad gave her a look, but Mom ignored him and took my chin in her hand, turning my head so I was looking right in her eyes. "You do what you want to do, Lucas. Think about what you really want here." The tears were running down her cheeks, but she didn't even try to wipe them away.

"I want him not to be dead," I said.

"I know, sweetie, me too. More than anything."

I can't remember what I didn't see. I didn't go in to see Charlie that night because Mom told me he wasn't there anymore. It was just his body. When I thought about that, his body lying cold under a sheet, I didn't want to go in and see anything that would replace my memories of him with something cold and lifeless.

The next few weeks were blurry, but not a blur the way it is when time goes fast. Everything slowed down. A lot of people showing up and saying sorry and Dad spending a lot of time outside chopping wood, which was something he did sometimes for extra money. Mom moved around the Box wrapped up in the quilt from Charlie's bed. Sometimes she was crying on the couch or in his room or, worst of all, in her own bed, where I guess she must have thought no one could hear her, because that was when she cried the loudest of all.

And the stuff I thought about was either too sad—

memories that made me want to double over because the pain was so bad—or too selfish, like wondering if it mattered at all to Mom that she had another kid.

The thing about when someone dies is that eventually time just starts moving at the regular speed again. And you think that the sad parts have healed, but they really haven't. It's like a cut where the scab forms on top, because that's just what scabs do, but underneath it's the same cut, just as open and painful as ever. The first day when I went back to school was the worst, because even though everyone was really nice to me, it was so obvious that they just wanted to keep moving on with their day and have everything be the same as if no one they loved was ever going to die.

When Mom went back to work, it was like she put on a mask, and when she came home and took off her work sneakers—the ones with the extra-supportive insoles—she took off her mask, too. Then Dad and I walked around the Box pretending like we couldn't hear her crying. Some nights were better: she would sit on the couch with me while I watched TV and run her hand through my hair or rub my back while she stared through the screen I knew she wasn't actually watching, because when I tried to talk to her about something that was happening on my show, she never had any idea what I was talking about.

Charlie had been gone before. He'd left for college and didn't even live with us anymore. I'd missed him a lot that first semester when he was gone, and I'd noticed how Mom and Dad talked to each other differently when he wasn't around. But once he was dead, I realized how good things had really been, because when someone was dead they weren't just gone from the world around you, they were somehow gone from the world inside you too.

CHAPTER 17

AFTER SCHOOL THE NEXT DAY ROBBIE FILLED HIS ACORN jar. He didn't look happy about it, though. He looked nervous, even though the rest of us were excited to have a crack at another wish.

"My wish is about Greg Hutchins," he said. "I want him to go away and never come back." He turned his face up toward the trees, like he had caught sight of something, but I could tell he was trying not to cry. His face was pale, and he was biting down hard on his lower lip.

"Well, we probably can't kill him," Cat joked, but none of us laughed. No one knew what to say. It was his wish. He had a right to his wish, even if we had no clue how to handle it.

"What does he do?" Cat asked.

Robbie took a deep breath and let it out in choppy little bursts. "Stupid stuff," he said. "Like whenever he sees me, he burps and blows it in my face if he's close enough. Or he waits until no one is looking and shoves me. Not hard or anything, but just enough to knock me off balance or make me drop stuff. And then he laughs. And all his stupid friends laugh."

"They're all afraid of him too," Anna said, looking down at her hands in her lap.

Robbie shook his head. "Well, they don't act like they're afraid of him. It's so bad now that if I even see him or any of his friends laughing, I just think they're laughing about me. Even if they're not. I start wondering what stupid thing I did that they're laughing at."

"What about a teacher?" Anna asked.

"Teachers?" Robbie sneered. "If they say anything, then Greg just acts like we're buddies. Like it's all good between us and we're just joking around. And I know if I ever said anything different, he'd make it even worse for me somehow. Besides," he added, looking down at his hands, "part of me wants to believe it too. That we're actually friends and it's all a joke. Because then I don't hate myself as much for being such a loser."

I was holding my breath. These things that Robbie was saying, I knew them all so well. I took a deep breath. "I'm afraid of him too!" I blurted out. When I looked up I saw that Anna and Robbie were nodding too.

"He's a bully," said Anna. "Like a real bully. And that's what he wants. He wants everyone to be afraid of him. It's kind of sad, really."

"I'm not afraid of him," Cat said. "He's a punk. I bet I could take him too, but he'd never fight a girl."

"Thanks," Robbie said, "but I don't think that would fix anything. No offense."

Cat shrugged.

Finn put his hands together so his palms and fingertips were touching. "Well, what are we going to do?"

"Nothing," Robbie said despondently. "I don't even know why I said anything or why I kept filling this stupid jar. There's nothing *we* can do that will make it better."

"You wouldn't have wished it if you really thought that," said Anna.

Robbie shrugged.

"Let's change our perspective," Finn said. We all lay back with our heads in the middle and stared up at the sky like we had before. "What is his raison d'être?"

"Huh?" Robbie said.

"What does Greg want?"

"To be a jerk," Robbie said.

"Yeah, but what does he really want?"

"What do you mean?" Cat said.

"I mean, no one is a jerk for no reason. What is the driving force behind his malevolence, his iniquity, his jerkiness," Finn said.

"I never did anything to him," Robbie burst out. "I swear."

"Of course you didn't. That's not the way his sort operates. But anger begets anger, so our villain is angry about something. We just have to figure out what it is."

"Like maybe someone was mean to him, so he's mean?" Robbie said. "How are we going to fix that? I'm not a guidance counselor. He's not going to talk to any of us about his problems. *He's* the problem."

"He's rotten," Finn agreed. "Not that it's much consolation, but I'm sure he feels rotten too."

"What does Greg have to feel bad about?" Robbie said bitterly. "He's good at sports and everyone likes him."

"He's not *that* good at sports," Cat said.

"Everyone pretends to like him," Anna said.

"Same difference," Robbie said.

Finn sat straight up. "That's what we need to know,"

he said. "We must conduct a study of Greg Hutchins. We need to figure out what he has to feel bad about, and then we exploit it to get him to stop picking on Robbie."

"Is that going to work?" Robbie asked.

"That sounds kind of mean," Anna said. "He's not my friend. Not really, anyway. But it sounds like we'd be doing back to him what he's doing to Robbie. And then what if it gets worse?"

"Maybe *exploit* was the wrong word," Finn said. "How about *gently manipulate*?"

"That's better, I guess," Anna said.

"Evil genius," I whispered.

"What did you say?" Finn asked.

I coughed and cleared my throat. "Evil genius." I ventured a look up at Robbie.

He smiled back.

CHAPTER 18

IT'S HARD TO FIGURE OUT A BULLY. I TRIED TO IMAGINE what Charlie would have said, but before he died, I didn't have middle school problems. In elementary school everyone in the class got a Valentine's card or a cupcake on someone's birthday because the teachers handed out those lists with every single name on it. If there were rules in middle school, they resembled Darwin's theory of survival of the fittest. Charlie had had lots of friends, but we'd never really talked about friend stuff. Maybe I would have turned out more like him if he'd been there to guide me. Now I was stuck just trying to figure out everything on my own.

Usually Dad left for work before me, rushing to make coffee and get out the door. But a couple days later he got up when I got up and didn't seem to be rushing at all. In fact, he was even humming as he made his coffee, so I took a risk and asked him something that had been on my mind.

"Did you have a lot of friends when you were my age?"

Instantly the humming stopped. "Yeah," he said, "I was friends with everybody."

"It's just that Mom always talks about Asher or Lucinda Swans from the market, but you never really do. Talk about your friends, I mean."

Dad shrugged. "I guess I just let it go. I mean, we were kids. Besides, I've never been really good at staying in touch with people."

I thought about this on the way to school. It was true: Dad didn't do Facebook or any of that other stuff that older people did on their phones. But I didn't believe him—at least, I didn't believe that what he was telling me was the whole truth.

For two days we watched Greg. And at the end of each day we met in the tree fort with nothing but boring little details to report.

"He goes to the bathroom every day at the same time during science," Cat volunteered.

"Is it after lunch?" Finn asked.

"Yeah."

"Well, regular peristalsis of the lower intestine is enough to embarrass some people, but I don't think it's enough for Greg Hutchins."

Greg was always the first one in the lunch line, either because he got there first or because he cut the line. He went to his classes and did his homework most of the time. He wasn't a good student, but he wasn't the worst, either. I thought we had hit a dead end. Maybe the thing with Cat was a fluke. I mean, how could acorn caps grant wishes anyway?

It could have been luck, or fate, or whatever you want to call it. But as soon as I saw that Mrs. Lynch was going to call on people to read the parts in our *Diary of Anne Frank* dramatization, I raised my hand for a pass to the bathroom, figuring she would have all the parts given out by the time I got back.

When I left the room, Greg Hutchins was standing outside the classroom across the hall, being spoken to by a teacher I didn't know. I could tell he'd done something bad by the way he kept looking at the floor and the ceiling. I walked past as slowly as possible, heading to the bathroom. I heard the teacher say, "I understand you're frustrated when you're reading, but you can't distract other students from getting their work done." Greg's face was red and kind of blotchy.

On the way back from the bathroom I saw he was still outside the classroom, sitting in a chair, scowling and kicking at a pen cap just a little bit out of his reach. I must have stared a second too long. "What's your problem, Puke-ass?" he spat at me. I looked quickly down but veered too sharply to the left and caught the edge of the lockers with my shoulder. Greg laughed, and my face burned as I walked back to class. My embarrassment faded quickly; I thought I might have something we could use.

"What's in room 256?" I asked when we were all in the tree fort. "Across from Mrs. Lynch's room."

"I think that's a Special Ed. room," Cat said. "My friend has English class in there. She's always bragging about how they don't have any homework. They have a teacher help them write their essays during class."

"Well, Greg has English in there," I said. I took a deep breath. "And I think he might have problems reading."

"Huh," Anna said. "That kind of makes sense. You know, I've seen him make some easy mistakes before. Like when he asked me if *Hatchet* was a book about chickens. He thought it said *hatched*. And I saw his test in social studies once and it wasn't the same as mine. He had a lot less questions." She paused. "We can't make fun of him for not being able to read," she said. "That's cruel."

"No," Finn said slowly. "That wouldn't really solve the problem anyway. But it does give me an idea." He twisted his baseball-bat pen back and forth between his fingers. Then suddenly he stopped. "Can everyone bring lunch from home tomorrow?"

Finn took the lid off one of the jars to represent the lunch table and placed five acorn caps around it for the five of us and a bent old bottle cap in the sixth position for Greg. Then he began to explain the plan.

Finn said we had three things going for us. We had numbers, we had the element of surprise, and now we had leverage. In order to make the plan work, we had to all get to lunch a little early in order to secure the table. Since we couldn't depend on the teachers to let us out early, we all agreed to sign out for a bathroom pass about five minutes before lunch started. Instead of coming back to class, we would go straight to the cafeteria and stake out our spots.

I woke up early the next morning, my mind already reviewing the details of the day's plan. I always got lunch at the cafeteria because Mom had filled out a form that meant we got it for free, and there wasn't much to choose from at home. I put a few pieces of sliced cheese in a bag along with some pretzels. I didn't think it was going to matter. I was already too nervous to eat breakfast, and it wasn't going to get any better.

At five minutes before lunch I raised my hand to ask for the pass, but Mr. Bennett was in the middle of a long story about the Vietnam War, which was sort of interesting but had nothing to do with our unit on ancient Mesopotamia. I stared at the second hand edging closer and closer to lunch. If I couldn't get there in time, I was going to ruin it for everyone.

He stopped class a minute before the bell and I practically exploded out of my seat and sprinted down the hall. When I got to the cafeteria, everyone else was already in their places. I barely had time to get to my assigned spot near the rack of chips by the cash registers when Greg Hutchins came through with his tray of pizza and chicken fries. I was sure everyone around me could hear the thudding of my heart against my rib cage.

Greg didn't hesitate. He went straight to his regular table, the table he sat at with a rotating cast of the popular kids. You could only sit six to a table, and the seats were first come, first served, but Greg never lost his seat. As soon as he sat down, we swept in.

I might have been half a step behind everyone else. I just didn't want to be the first one to sit down. I was afraid that if Greg said something to me, I would lose my nerve.

"What the—" Greg had a chicken fry dripping with ketchup half in and half out of his mouth as we all plunked ourselves down at the table. A blob of ketchup fell out of his mouth and landed with a splat on the blue plastic tray.

"Hello, Greg," Finn said casually, as if we always sat together. He opened his crinkled brown paper bag and took out a sandwich neatly sealed in a ziplock bag. Anna opened her purple flowered lunch bag and pulled out some sliced fruit, a sandwich, and a small bag of cookies. I thought I saw her hands shaking. I was supposed to eat—that was the plan. I pulled out the bag of pretzels and managed to stick one piece in my mouth, letting the saliva slowly turn it to mush, too nervous to chew.

Greg stood up and picked up his tray. I looked around for one of the teachers who monitored lunch. You weren't allowed to change seats once you sat down, I guess to keep kids from running all over the place. He hesitated for a second. Getting caught switching seats meant you had to suffer a week of lunch detention at the teacher's table. But if no one saw him? "Sit down, Greg." It was Anna. Her voice was different: stronger and more confident. I didn't know what *her* mother sounded like, but she sounded like somebody's mother for sure.

Greg scowled, but he sat back down. The cafeteria was

filling up now. A few of Greg's friends started over to his table but turned away, with confused expressions on their faces, when they saw all of us sitting there. "Whatever," he said, and went back to his food, eating quickly, as if that would make the lunch period go faster.

Cat reached into her backpack and pulled out two cans of root beer. She slid one around to Anna and one to Robbie. Then she pulled out two more, kept one, and gave the other to me. I opened mine and took a few big gulps. Everyone else did the same. Greg's upper lip curled into a sneer, but he didn't say anything. Finally, when the cafeteria was almost full and the noise was at its loudest, Finn spoke again.

"We've got a problem, Greg," he said.

"So?" Greg said.

That was our cue. Cat went first. She let out a huge burp. "Oooooooo-wahhhhhhhh!" It came out low and rattly. Some kids turned to look, and there were some giggles from the tables around us. Then Robbie let go a stuttering series of burps. I could tell he was nervous, because he wasn't looking up at any of us. Then me. I swigged the soda again and produced a respectably loud, punchy burp. Since I hadn't eaten anything, the root beer left a sickly-sweet flavor in the back of my throat. Greg looked confused, then just plain disgusted. Finally, Anna took a deep breath and burped. It was loud *and* gurgly. Several girls at the surrounding tables turned and stared, open-mouthed.

"What the hell?" Greg said. "You guys are sick." He picked up another chicken fry and tried to pretend like nothing was going on.

"Isn't it, though?" Finn said. He was taking neat little bites of his sandwich. According to our plan, he was the one who was supposed to do all the talking. "Robbie thinks it's pretty disgusting too. Funny the two of you have that in common." Robbie suddenly pretended to be very interested in the crumbs at the bottom of his bag of chips.

"Whatever," Greg said.

"'Whatever' indeed!" Finn said. He seemed delighted, as though Greg had made an excellent point. Then he lowered his voice. "If 'whatever' means you're going to leave Robbie alone."

Greg looked up. "Or what?"

"As far as I can tell, he hasn't done anything to you. It's pretty small-minded of you to pick on someone just because of their last name or something else they can't help."

"Are you calling me dumb?" Greg's face became a mask of evil—like when Anakin Skywalker submits to the dark side. He probably practiced that look in the mirror: the one he gave kids before he made an appointment to find them after school and pound their internal organs into tomato sauce. I looked around for the nearest red exit sign. I caught one of the teachers staring at our table. It was Ms. Edgerly. She looked interested in what was going on, but she didn't come any closer.

"Of course not," Finn replied. "I would never pick on someone for something they couldn't do anything about." There was a tiny pause. Was he going for it?

"Like not being able to read," Anna said quietly. She wasn't supposed to say it, but it was kind of perfect coming from her. Anna was nice to everyone, and she was friends with all Greg's friends. Her words hit home perfectly.

Greg's cheeks turned bright red. Was he going to flip the table over? Smash us in the face with his lunch tray? No. Wait. Were those actual tears? Had the impossible really occurred—did Greg Hutchins have actual feelings? "Whatever, losers!" He stood up and stormed out of the cafeteria, missing the trash can with half the contents of his tray. I cringed as the teacher on lunch duty chased him down and made him pick up the trash he had dumped on the floor.

The cafeteria was hushed for a second after this display. A few people glanced nervously over at us, but then, just as quickly, the noise picked up again. Had we done it? I ventured a smile at Robbie, who smiled back more cautiously. My stomach let out a huge rumble, so I got up from my chair and went, with shaking hands, to get a sun butter and jelly sandwich, which was all that was left now that everyone had been through the line. Ms. Edgerly walked by me on my way back to our table, and I swear she smirked ever so slightly. The day was getting weirder and weirder.

After school Robbie and I kicked through the frozen leaves looking for acorn caps. "It seems greedy to keep looking," Robbie said. "I mean, I got my wish. This afternoon I saw Greg in between classes, and I swear he crossed to the other side of the hall to avoid me. It was like he was afraid of me! Of *me*?"

"Must feel better."

"Yeah!" Robbie said. "I mean, if it lasts that would be good too. But even if it doesn't, I'm glad I did something. I mean, we did something."

I was part of that "we." I was part of any "we." I took a deep breath. "Hey, um, if you had a birthday party, would you invite me?"

Robbie gave me a really strange look, and for a second I thought I had messed everything up. "Of course I would!" Then he looked down. "I didn't have a party last year. My mom took me to a hockey game in Boston instead, so that was like my whole present. And, well, my birthday's in January, so the year before . . ." His voice trailed off. "My mom said we shouldn't bother your family with a party, you know?"

I nodded. He could have been lying, I guess, but I didn't think he was. Robbie didn't seem like the type.

"So, it's two wishes down," he said.

"Yeah," I said. I had been thinking about how I could just dump all my acorn caps into Anna's jar. It was getting harder and harder to avoid filling mine up.

As if he could read my mind, Robbie said, "You know what the hardest part was?"

"Uh . . . uh . . ." I shook my head.

"It was telling you guys. I mean, it was freaky sitting across from Greg in the cafeteria and everything, but at least we did that together. It was way harder to admit to you guys that he was picking on me. It made me realize how really awful it was, and how much I wanted it to stop."

"Yeah," I said as I crushed an acorn cap under my shoe.

CHAPTER 19

THE PHONE RANG IN THE MIDDLE OF THE NIGHT. I STUM-
bled out of my room in my pj's and picked up the receiver.

"Hello?"

I heard a click and then nothing. It had to be Mom.

For the first few months after Charlie died, every time
the phone rang, I thought it would be him. I couldn't wait
to pick up the phone and hear him say my name the way
he always did, drawing out the *s* on the end so it sounded
like a snake hissing. And every time it wasn't him, it was
like getting kicked in the stomach. But what was worse
was when it stopped. One day the phone just rang, and I
didn't even pay attention.

This was different, though. Mom wasn't dead. Had

she wished she were? That was a terrifying thought. Mom didn't talk about being sad. She went back to work and made dinner for us again. But something was different. She looked nervous and worried a lot of the time. She twisted her hands in her lap or picked at her nails when we watched TV together. She didn't laugh and her voice sounded sad when we read together, and not just at the sad parts.

I'd picked up the receiver only to hear her hang up. I hadn't even gotten to imagine I could hear her breathing. I hadn't even gotten to shout, "Where the heck are you?" I slid to the floor and leaned back against the wall. I could feel the cold metal floor beneath the thin layer of carpet. The walls were thin enough that the whole place shook in a storm or even if a big truck went by on nearby Route 77. I could picture the dark crawl space beneath the rug and the floor and my butt. I wrapped my arms around my knees, thinking that there was practically nothing between me and the cold world.

A fat tear slid out of the corner of my eye and dangled for a minute on the end of my nose before pooling on the knuckles of my left hand. And then another and another, and I let my shoulders shake and big sobs come out from that place below your ribs where the worst crying comes from. Part of me hoped Dad would wake up and maybe he would be so mad about me crying and waking him up in the middle of the night that he would hit me, and I'd have to run out of the house and find our landlord, Mr. Boudreau. I'd have to tell him everything that was going on and he would know what to do with a kid like me.

Then I felt angry. Angry at myself for thinking I had it bad. Like anyone would care or do anything about it. Mad overtook sad. I stopped crying and stood up. Dad's snores shook the Box. I was alone, just being sad and mad at everyone. I wanted to do something, anything, so everyone would know how mad and sad I really was. So I went to the fridge and took out a couple of Dad's precious beers. I pulled down Dad's heavy work coat from the hook beside the door and slipped a bottle into each pocket before I stepped out into the night.

The air on my legs was freezing. I looked around, and then, without really thinking about where I was going at midnight in Dad's coat and my pajamas, I stalked off into the woods.

In the darkness the trailer boxes were dark rectangles between the trees. I pulled one of the beers out of my pocket. Keeping my hand inside the sleeve of Dad's coat, I twisted the top off until it hissed. I sniffed and recoiled at the smell. How did anyone drink this stuff? This was what Dad wanted at the end of a long day—"to take the edge off" was what he liked to say. I was nothing but edges. It wasn't fair. I turned the bottle over and listened as the liquid glug-glugged out of the bottle and spattered on the leaves below.

For a moment it was satisfying, but then I felt worse. I thought about how sometimes Dad had to scrape together change in the truck to buy himself a Coke or a pack of gum for me. I couldn't remember the last time he'd had new clothes or even a new pair of boots for work. He was part of the problem, but he wasn't the whole thing.

I crept back into the house, slid the full bottle back in the fridge, and hid the empty one in my backpack. I could find a dumpster to toss it in after school. I climbed into bed, fell asleep, and slept soundly. But as soon as I woke up, I knew something was wrong. My head felt heavy and hot, and when I shed my blankets and stood up, I started to shake and shiver. I went to the bathroom and then crawled back into bed. The light hurt my eyes, so I closed them and drifted in and out of a hot, uncomfortable sleep.

Dad poked his head in before he left for work. I squinted at him, my eyes just barely peeking out of the covers. "You all right?" he asked.

"Uh-uh," I said.

"Feeling sick?"

"Yeah."

"Like you're going to puke? You want a bucket?"

"I don't think so," I whispered.

"Well, if you're going to puke, try and make it to the toilet."

Geez, thanks, Dad, I thought. You're a real Florence Nightingale.

"You can stay home, I guess," he said. "I gotta go." He waited for a minute. "You'll be all right?" It was only sort of a question.

"Yeah," I said.

He looked around like he was trying to think of what else to offer me. "There's some cold medicine in the cabinet, I think. If you're really sick, you can call me at the shop."

"Okay."

Then he was gone. I heard the door close behind him and the truck engine roar to life. Then it was quiet. Mom always stayed with me at least until she had to work the lunch shift. I pulled the covers all the way over my head and drifted off.

When I woke up, I felt a little better, so I wrapped myself up in my blankets and relocated in front of the TV. There were game shows on, so I watched those and stared out the window when the commercials came on. Around noon my stomach came to life, grumbling and reminding me that I hadn't eaten anything. I made myself a package of ramen noodles and ate them in front of old *SpongeBob* episodes. I left the bowl and the dirty pot in the sink and crawled back into my bedroom.

I woke up again late in the afternoon with an awful metallic taste in my mouth. I brushed my teeth and put on a clean T-shirt before wrapping back up in my blankets. The sun was low in the sky and there were talk shows on TV, which I watched mindlessly while eating some stale crackers until Dad came home. I saw him eye the dirty dishes in the sink before dropping some grocery bags on the kitchen table.

"You want some soup?" he asked, thunking a heavy can on the table.

"Sure."

"I wasn't sure what was wrong, so I got some stuff." He pulled out a bottle of juice—real Tropicana, not the store-brand kind—and some Pepto-Bismol. He put the juice in the refrigerator and shoved the rest of the groceries onto one of our shelves. I had a glass of orange juice and a can of chicken noodle soup for dinner.

I knew Dad was feeling bad about leaving me all day,

because he didn't even try to change the channel. Before I went to bed he said, kind of gruffly, "You can take care of those dishes in the morning." I nodded without looking back.

The next morning Dad woke me up by shaking my shoulder. "You think you can go to school today?"

It took a few seconds for me to realize he was giving me a choice. Mom never did that. She would take my temperature, feel my forehead—which she claimed was nearly as accurate—and most of the time hustle me out of bed and onto the bus. I squinted somewhat dramatically, as if I could hardly see him standing in front of me, and shook my head. Taking advantage of my froggy morning voice, I croaked out a no.

"Okay," Dad said, and he left it at that.

That day, school called. I picked up the phone since I was the only one home.

"Good morning," the voice on the other end chirped. "This is Mrs. Kelley from Feltzer Harding Middle School. Is Mr. or Mrs. Barnes at home?"

"No."

"Is this Lucas?"

"Yes," I said before considering where the truth would get me.

"Lucas, you've been reported truant, honey. Are you sick?"

"Yes." My heart started pounding in my chest so loudly, I thought for sure she would hear it through the phone.

"Well, your parents really need to call the school and let us know. Otherwise we're going to have to send Officer Bob out to your house." Officer Bob was the school resource police officer, a guy with a skinny mustache who liked to walk around during lunch and show kids like Greg Hutchins his handcuffs and Taser.

"Okay," I said, "I'll make sure they call."

There was a pause on the line. "Well, are you okay, honey?"

"Yeah," I said. "I mean no." My brain scanned my twelve years of experience of kid illness for something that would keep me out but not kill me or elicit any kind of weird pity campaign from the guidance office. "I might have mono."

"Oh no," Mrs. Kelley said appreciatively.

"They're not sure yet," I said. "And I could be contagious, so . . ."

"Okay," Mrs. Kelley said. "Well, we'll need to hear from your parents tomorrow. Or we'll have to mark you as having an unexcused absence."

"Okay," I said. "Is that all?" I'd meant was the phone call over, but Mrs. Kelley took it a different way.

"Well, it does go on your permanent record," she said,

sounding a little put out.

"Oh." I wasn't sure what to say. What did your permanent record for sixth grade look like, anyway? "Well, I should probably go lie down now."

Mrs. Kelley's voice got kind of sugary again and she said, "Okay, honey, feel better soon."

I hung up the phone.

The next day when the phone rang, I didn't answer it. I figured if it was Dad, I would just say I'd been sleeping, and if Officer Bob really did show up at my house, what was he going to do? Drag me to school in my pajamas? Besides, it was Friday, and I didn't really see the point of going back to school for one day before the weekend.

CHAPTER 20

SATURDAY WAS LAUNDRY DAY, AND DAD'S PATIENCE WITH
me being sick was over. He woke me up with a loud rapping
on my door and told me to get my clothes together and
meet him out by the truck. I stuffed everything I had into
an olive-green duffel bag. I pulled on my last clean pair of
boxers and a not-so-clean pair of jeans, brushed my teeth,
and headed out to the truck.

"You're feeling better," Dad said.

I just nodded. It wasn't like he even said it like a real
question.

Across from the Laundromat was a bar that stayed open
at weird hours. Dad put in the wash and then left me there
while he went across the street. I wandered around the

Laundromat, picking up any reading material that might be remotely interesting. The town weekly took only about seven minutes to read, even with all the boring classifieds.

After that there was half a ripped *People* magazine and the *Boston Globe* sports section. I played on my DS for a while until the batteries died, which they always did because it was so old. It had actually been Charlie's. Then I just lay down across a bunch of the plastic seats, let my head dangle backward over the end, and watched the soapy laundry swish back and forth inside the metal cylinder. There was only one other person sitting in the Laundromat that morning: an older woman knitting something maroon and shapeless. I could feel her glaring at me when I put my feet up on the seats, but I didn't really care.

I swished my head back and forth with the rhythm of the sudsy water. I was almost getting sleepy when I heard familiar voices. I shot up and then just as quickly ducked back down. Anna Perkins and her mother were walking quickly down the sidewalk. Their voices were loud and angry. I slid up to the window nearest to where they were standing, but I still couldn't make out any full sentences, just something about friends and reputations. The knitting lady scowled at me as if she knew what I was trying to do.

I waited a minute or so after their voices faded and then

scooted out the door and down the sidewalk in the same direction. Anna was walking slowly behind her mother, her head down. Her mother grabbed a cart from in front of the supermarket and pushed it through the automatic door, which swung open just a split second before she would have crashed through it. The whole time, she had her phone pinned between her shoulder and her ear.

I followed them into the store and stood at the end of the aisle and watched as Anna tossed things into the cart only to have her mother discard half of them without even looking to see what they were. A few times she picked up an item, appeared to read the label, and then put it back on the shelf. Anna just kept adding things and her mother kept taking them out. She wasn't on her phone talking any longer, but I could hear it beeping and sending out notifications. When I peeked around the corner at the end of the toilet paper aisle, Anna was gone and it was only her mom standing there, staring down into her phone like it was Dumbledore's Pensieve. I felt a light tap on my shoulder and whirled around to see Anna standing there with a smug look on her face.

"Hi," she said.

"Hi."

"Are you spying on me?"

"No!" I started to stammer out excuses, but Anna smiled and shook her head.

"Well, what are you doing?"

"Laundry."

"In the grocery store?"

"Uh, we needed soap."

"Oh," Anna said. "Well, where have you been?"

"I was sick."

"For practically a whole week? You don't look sick."

I shrugged. "I'm better now." I was starting to blush, and even though I tried not to, I started pulling on the front of my sweatshirt.

"Well, it's kind of sucked this week. Since you haven't been there."

"What do you mean?" Did she mean like in the time I wasn't there, or *because* I wasn't there?

Anna rolled her eyes. "Hang on a minute. Are you done here?" I nodded. "Good." She shouted down the aisle, "Mom, I'm going to help Lucas with his laundry."

Mrs. Perkins barely looked up as she waved Anna away.

"We'll be in the Laundromat next door," she shouted over her shoulder. I just followed, feeling the light pressure of her fingernails on my arm. "Where's your soap?" she said as we walked out of the store empty-handed.

"My dad took it," I mumbled. "I was just bored, walking around and stuff."

This much lying was easier than I thought it would be, but more nerve-racking too.

When we got back to the Laundromat, she jumped up and sat on one of the counters. Our machines had stopped so I grabbed a cart and started pulling the wet clothes out.

"It's kind of cool in here," Anna said, looking around. The knitting lady was gone, but there were a couple of teenagers in one corner sharing a pair of earbuds and nodding along to the same music. "Like, grown up. Your dad lets you do this all by yourself?"

"Sometimes. He's across the street running an errand." It wasn't completely a lie.

Anna hopped down and grabbed something out of my cart before I could stop her. "What's this?"

She was holding up one of the many blue short-sleeve button-up shirts my dad wore to work—each with his name embroidered in red over the left chest pocket.

"It's one of my dad's work shirts."

"Oh, it's kind of cool." She held it up and then pressed it forward toward me. "It could be like retro." She held it closer, like she was sizing it up for me to wear. "And the blue would look good with your eyes."

My face got hot and I grabbed more wet laundry, turning away to stuff it in the dryer. Anna got back up on the counter, chewing her gum and swinging her feet. "Anyway," she said, "like I was saying. It's been really bad this week without you. I filled my jar, and no one knows how to solve my problem. Yesterday Robbie didn't even come outside. He said he had too much homework." She rolled her eyes.

"What does that have to do with me?" I asked quietly.

"I don't know. It's just different when you're not there. You're like the center of things. What's that called at the middle of a wheel?"

"The hub?"

"Yeah, the hub. Plus, you're the only one who really talks to Finn. I mean, I never know what to say to him. He's just different. And you always know how to talk to him."

It had never occurred to me that Finn was a difficult person to talk to. No more than anyone else, at least for me. Maybe he was hard to understand at times because he used weird words that nobody else did, but I just ignored that part.

"So, what's your problem?" I said.

"Huh? Oh," she said, "*that* problem. You saw her. Everything about her is my problem: the way she acts, the way she talks to me. But mostly the way she *doesn't* talk to me. She barely sees me. It's like unless I'm in the way of her getting work done somehow, I'm invisible." She looked down at her swinging feet. "Completely invisible."

I knew about invisible. But I didn't think that my invisible and Anna's invisible were quite the same thing.

"We'll figure something out." I tried to meet her eyes so she would know that I wasn't just saying it, that I really meant it. But Anna was staring out the window, a faraway look on her face.

"Yeah, well, you'll be there Monday, right?"

"Yes."

"Good." She jumped down from the counter. "I should probably get back to the store so my mom doesn't freak out about me wasting her time."

I nodded, but I didn't want her to go. "What were you arguing about?" I blurted out.

Anna scowled and looked uncomfortable. "She heard from Nicole's mom that I wasn't being very social or whatever with my friends. And that I was hanging out with a bunch of weird kids after school instead of doing my homework." She held up air quotes when she said the word *weird*. "She has no clue. She started lecturing me about how things are different for me and I can't always expect to get second chances."

I was quiet, wondering if Anna's mother was a little bit right. Anna stepped toward me and said, "She's wrong, Lucas. I mean, not about everything, but she's wrong about you guys. She doesn't even know you, and if she did, she'd know you're not the wrong kind of people she's worried about. Just because they're grown-ups doesn't mean they always do or say the right thing." I looked away, because I had my doubts, even though I really wanted to believe what she was saying.

I slammed the dryer door and dropped in some quarters, and the machine started with a big whooshing noise.

"I should go. See you Monday, right?" she said, emphasizing the last word, and walked out the door. Once she was gone, I sat down hard on one of the plastic chairs. My hands were shaking. The whole conversation, my first real conversation alone with a girl, had me shaking.

CHAPTER 21

WHEN I GOT IN THE SHOWER ON MONDAY MORNING, THE smell of Mom was gone. The hot water used to stir up the citrusy smells of the shampoo she used. But that morning it just smelled like our slightly mildewed plastic-walled shower stall. I squeezed her nearly empty shampoo bottle, sending a few glassy bubbles into the steam, but it wasn't Mom. It just smelled like the shampoo aisle at the drugstore.

I was still thinking about her as I got dressed and when I poured the last of the cereal into my bowl. Dad was drinking coffee and looking at his phone.

"I want to visit Mom," I said.

Dad looked up at me, and immediately a deep crease formed between his eyebrows. "Lucas, we've talked about this."

"No, we haven't," I said. "Not really."

"Well, you can't."

"Why not?"

"Because, I told you already." Dad was getting flustered. "She's getting better. They're helping her, and when she's ready, she'll call you."

The truth hit me like a sledgehammer to the gut. "You haven't talked to her either," I said softly. "Do you even know where she is?"

Dad slammed down his coffee cup and turned away. He picked up and put down some papers on the counter. Then he stood at the counter staring out the window for a minute.

"Her voicemail is full."

"Well, can you call Aunt Sheila?"

Dad looked at me like I'd suggested he clean the toilet with his toothbrush. "It's not that simple," he said. But something in my face must have changed his mind, because he added, "I'll see what I can do, Lucas, but I'm not promising anything." He took another sip of his coffee and glared at me like it was my fault it had gone cold. But it wasn't my fault, and neither was asking about Mom, even if it made him think about stuff he didn't want to think about, or do stuff he didn't want to do.

Before I left, I snuck one of Dad's blue work shirts into my backpack, and when I got on the bus, I pulled it on over my plain gray T-shirt, feeling a like a bit of an impostor. But when I got to school, I walked past Mrs. Kelley, who called out to me, "Lucas, are you feeling better?"

"Yes."

"Well, you look better. You look very nice today."

I murmured a thank-you, tugged at the front of my shirt, and walked to my locker. When I saw Anna in the hall, she didn't say anything, but she looked right at the pocket of my shirt and smiled really big.

In the middle of second period, it started to snow. Big, chunky flakes fell from the sky, glopping on the trees and blanketing the ground with a thick white coating. By third period all after-school sports had been canceled. Everyone was excited about the first real snowstorm and the possibility of a snow day.

Walking down to the cafeteria that afternoon, my backpack was straining against my shoulders with the weight of pretty much every book and binder I had. I had a ton of makeup work to do from the time I was out, something I hadn't really thought about when I was sitting on the couch enjoying some *SpongeBob*. Slowly everyone else filed in, grabbed their carrots and individually sized cup of ranch dip, and opened up their books.

"Hi," I said to no one in particular.

Finn looked up. "The conquering hero returns."

I smiled back. I was really glad to see them, and I didn't remember ever feeling like that about coming to school before.

"I don't want to talk about problems today," Robbie said. He put his pencil down. He'd barely started the math worksheet we were supposed to do that night. "Let's play a game!"

"Like what?" Cat said.

"Capture the flag?" Robbie suggested.

"Yes!" Cat said. "Me, you, and Anna against those two."

I stared down at the pile of work I had to do that night. Playing outside was a lot more appealing. And if we did have a snow day, I'd have the whole day to catch up. "Okay, I'm in."

We found an old sweatshirt and bandanna from the lost and found to be our flags and pulled on our coats and hats. Steve looked at us like we were crazy. "You're going out in this?" The little kids were already getting out the Twister and the board games.

"We've been inside all day," Cat said.

And even though Louise looked like her eyes were

about to bug out of her head, Steve shrugged and said, "Suit yourselves."

Outside the school building it was eerily quiet. Even the teachers' parking lot was nearly empty. The gray skies and snow-covered ground made everything feel deserted and exciting—like we were the only survivors of a snowpocalypse. We walked into the woods, our boots and sneakers sinking softly into the new snow. I grabbed a handful off a pine bough. It crumpled and compacted in my hand, squeezing between my gloved fingers and holding its shape: decent enough for snowballs.

When we got to the clearing, Robbie laid out the rules.

"This is jail for both teams. A clear shot with a snowball is the only way to get someone. No guarding your flag. First team to capture the flag, bring it to the fort, and blow the air horn is the winner." The air horn was something Cat had found on the soccer field, left over from one of the games. We'd never had a chance to use it.

"When do we start?" I asked.

"I don't know. How about five minutes?" Robbie looked around at us. "Go!"

Finn and I took off running through the woods, back toward the dump and the fort. But after just a little bit, our feet were dragging in the snow, and Finn was wheezing behind me, so I slowed down.

"They'll expect us to go back this way," he said.

"Let's double back toward the school and find a tree to hide it in," I suggested.

Finn agreed, so as quietly as possible we snuck through the snow back toward the school, wrapping our tracks around the trees and stamping out little clearings as we went, to try to cover the exact path we were taking. We crammed the flag in one of the tall pines almost at the edge of the woods. There was nothing special about it, and that was what I liked. It blended right in with all the other trees. We had to leave the flag partially visible, because otherwise we'd be cheating.

"It's probably best to stay together so we'll know if one of us has to be rescued from jail. Maybe just a little bit apart. Like fifteen feet or so," I said. We marked off the distance and started through the snow back toward the clearing, where we hoped we might be able to follow the other team's trail.

The air in my nose and throat was cold, but I could taste the snow in it. My feet were going numb, but I didn't care. Then, just a few feet ahead of us, I saw shapes behind the trees. I flung myself down and signaled for Finn to do the same. The best part of capture the flag was pretending like you were really in a battle. I got up on one knee and began to press the snow together into the perfect snowball. As soon as it had a decent shape, I hurled it through the trees at the back of Robbie's hooded head.

"Ow! Hey, what the heck?" The voice was older— definitely not Robbie's.

There were two big kids, probably high school kids, standing there. The one I hit was shaking snow off the back of his sweatshirt. Robbie, Anna, and Cat were standing there too.

"Sorry," I said. "I thought you were someone else."

"Yeah," the kid said. "So did that guy."

I looked confused. "That's not a guy," Anna said.

"Oh, sorry," he said.

"Dude, Mitchell," his friend said. "You can't tell that's a girl?"

"I don't know, man; she looks weird."

Cat hunched up her shoulders as they started snickering.

"Shut up!" Anna said. Robbie and I muttered something that I hoped sounded like agreement but maybe not enough to get us beat up.

These kids were like a foot taller than us. But the guy called Mitchell didn't even seem to be listening. He just kept giggling, and then his phone blew up with like a thousand pings.

"Dude, turn that thing off."

"I'm driving her crazy, dude," Mitchell said, looking at his phone. "I got a new number, and now I can bug her as much as I want. She doesn't even know it's me!"

His friend looked annoyed. "I thought you said you were over her!"

"Yeah," Mitchell said. "Exactly."

"You guys in middle school?"

We nodded.

"High school's lit. It's so much cooler."

Mitchell was tapping something into his phone and giggling. He didn't look so much cooler. His eyes were all squinty and he smelled weird. The other guy pushed him and said, "Come on, man, we gotta bounce."

"Hey," Mitchell said, "you messed me up."

"Whatever, man." Then he turned to us as he started out of the clearing. "See you later, kiddies."

We all looked at each other. I picked up a big handful of snow. Robbie grinned and quickly patted a ball into place. The first one I threw caught the bigger kid square in the back. Then we all started hurling snowballs, rapid-fire, one after another.

They yelled a few bad words, but they started running, and we kept throwing until we couldn't hear them any longer.

As soon as they were gone, I turned on Robbie with

a huge snowball right in the face. He looked mad for a second, but then he bent down and scooped up a huge pile of snow in his mittens. "Take cover!" I yelled to Finn. We ran a few feet and ducked behind a big rock. Finn began to make snowballs, and I pumped them in the direction of Robbie, Anna, and Cat. But we were outnumbered, and pretty soon they had us surrounded and we had to yield to a full-on whitewash.

Finn yelped and hollered, and when we were completely overwhelmed by snow, he lay on his back and flapped his arms and legs to make a snow angel. We all threw ourselves on the ground and did the same. I had to keep blinking to prevent the snow from piling up on my eyelashes and blinding me completely. When Finn stood up, he turned around to admire the shape he'd created in the snow. "I, Phineas Clark, was here!" he declared.

"It's going to get covered in like five minutes," Robbie said, looking at his own shape in the snow behind him.

"So it shall, so it shall," Finn agreed.

We trudged back toward the school, stamping our feet and slapping our hands against our bodies to shake off the snow and stay warm.

"Hey," Robbie said as I fell in to walk next to him. "Look what I found." He pulled what looked like part of a bone out of his jacket pocket. "It was poking up out of the snow back by the dump."

"Cool."

"I think it's a jaw."

"Oh yeah, I can kind of see a tooth there."

"Think Ms. Edgerly would know what it is?"

"I don't know. Maybe."

"Come with me to her room tomorrow and ask?"

"Why me?"

"She likes you."

I looked at Robbie like he had two heads. "She hates me!"

"Nah," he said. "You can tell she likes you."

"She was my brother Charlie's favorite teacher."

"Maybe you remind her of him, and it makes her sad," Robbie suggested. And, coming out of his mouth, it almost made sense—or it would have, if I were anything like Charlie.

"Maybe," I said.

"Well, whatever. Don't you want to know what it is? Maybe it's like the key to an unsolved murder."

"Of a deer?"

"Are you going to come or what?"

"Sure, fine, whatever."

I had something else on my mind. The high schoolers

had given me an idea—a crazy idea, maybe, but an idea that might help solve Anna's problem. When we got back to the cafeteria, Cat's mom was there waiting impatiently for Cat, and Steve was looking at us like he was annoyed that we were making him look bad. So the idea would have to wait until we were all together the next afternoon. I turned it over and over in my mind that night, like flipping a shiny quarter in my palm. Was it too crazy to work, or was it crazy perfect?

CHAPTER 22

"HEY, LUCAS, WAIT UP!"

Robbie caught me in the hall the next day after the dismissal bell. He was holding the jawbone he'd found in the woods. "Still going to come with me?" I didn't answer right away. I'd been counting the minutes until we got to the fort and I could tell everyone my idea to solve Anna's problem. "Come on," he said. "It will only take a minute."

I was half hoping Ms. Edgerly would be out of her room or in a meeting. But of course she was sitting at her desk in front of her computer when we came in.

"Hi, boys," she said when we walked in. "What's that?"

The first thing I noticed as we approached her desk was that up close she looked older. There were crinkly lines at the corners of her eyes. I scanned her desk, taking in the pictures of her on the beach, kayaking and hiking on top of some mountain, her arm wrapped around a friend; the box of tea; and the mason jar of honey that looked like someone had scooped it right out of a beehive.

Robbie put the jawbone down on her desk. "Do you think it's human?"

She smiled and then looked at him seriously. "Who did you boys kill?" Robbie took a step back and she laughed. "Uh, seriously, though, no. This is not human. Lucas, why not?"

"Um, not enough teeth?"

She smiled. "Yes, and?"

"It's not the right shape. It's too long and, um, snouty."

Ms. Edgerly smiled again. "Not quite a scientific term, but I know exactly what you mean. Definitely too snouty to be human." She picked it up and turned it over. "Your victim was most likely a deer. See these flat teeth—well, tooth? This animal was a bark chewer, not a meat ripper."

Robbie looked a little disappointed. But Ms. Edgerly seemed excited about it. "Are you going to keep it? If you don't want it, can I have it?"

"Sure," Robbie said, "you can have it."

Ms. Edgerly got up from behind her desk and went over to a shelf that had other bones, some smooth rocks perfectly bisected by lines of quartz, seashells, and a stick covered with rows of perfectly aligned little holes. "I've got a collection—former students, etcetera." She paused again. "Kidding, guys."

"Cool," Robbie said, and he picked up one of the rocks. It was completely black except for a sparkly white line of quartz running in a perfect circle around the middle.

I turned over a thick piece of white shell in my hand. It was perfectly ridged with horizontal lines on one side. When I flipped it over, the other side was cloudy with black and gray swirls. I turned it back and forth in my hand. When I looked up, Ms. Edgerly was giving me a funny look.

"Geez," she said softly.

"What is it?" I asked.

"A piece of a quahog shell, I think," she said. "I found it on a beach walk and I liked the feel of it in my hand." Just then one of our school custodians poked her head in. Ms. Edgerly looked up. That pained look was on her face again. "We're done here," she called out abruptly. The woman in the gray work shirt smiled and nodded. "Anyway, you boys should probably get going. I've got an appointment, and they've got to clean the room." But she watched me as I reluctantly put the shell down. I didn't like letting go of it.

When we got to the door, she called after us. "Hang on

just a second, boys." She paused, glancing at Robbie and then back at me. She seemed uncertain about whatever she was going to say. "That was Charlie's favorite too." Hearing her say his name opened up a funny little pit in my stomach. "He used to hold that shell in his hand every day in class. He said it helped him focus." She smiled sadly. "I probably should have given it to him. He had a thing he used to say about it. Something about the different sides. I can't remember. If I think of it, I'll tell you."

"Okay," I said.

"Okay," she said back.

I left the room, but my finger twitched, trying to remember the feel of the shell in my hand. Charlie's hand had been there too.

"I think we would get caught," Anna said, wide-eyed.

"Yeah, that sounds illegal," Robbie said.

"I don't think it's illegal," I mumbled.

Everyone was quiet. "What if they traced the calls?" Cat asked.

"That's why we would use a prepaid cell phone," I said. I looked around and realized they didn't know what I was talking about. "You can get them at Walmart. Sometimes they even sell them at gas stations. They're just like regular cell phones, except they don't have data plans or contracts or anything. Anyone can get one, and then you just use it until your minutes are up. You can add more minutes, I think, but you might need a credit card for that. Anyway, we wouldn't be making any calls, just sending texts." I looked at Anna. "You said it's the only thing your mom pays attention to, right?"

Anna nodded.

"What would the texts say?" Robbie asked.

I shrugged.

"*I* know what they would say," Anna said, her eyes gleaming. "How are we going to get money for the phone?"

"I've got some birthday money saved up," Robbie said.

"We could all give some money," Cat suggested. I looked away.

"I'll procure the phone," Finn said. "We stop at Walmart frequently."

"Won't your parents think that's weird?" Anna asked.

Finn gave a little snort that sounded as close to anger as I'd ever heard him get. "Unlikely," he said.

"You'll have to send them at night," Anna said. "Otherwise she'll think I'm the one doing it."

"What time?" I asked.

"Probably between six and seven. That's around when

she gets home. Usually I finish my homework in the kitchen and she's heating up whatever is for dinner. I mean, when she's not on her phone."

"Don't do it at your house," Robbie said. "I saw that on a crime show once. They can trace where the phone calls come from. They, like, bounce the signal off cell phone towers and satellites and stuff."

"Really?" Cat said.

"I could walk down the street," Finn said.

"Yeah," Robbie agreed. "Or maybe we should all take turns sending the messages. That way they're coming from all over the place." His eyes got really wide. "We can hand off the phone by leaving it in a waterproof bag inside the toilet tank at school!"

"Ew!" we chorused.

"I think we can find another way to hand off the phone and safely avoid both suspicion and bacterial infection," Finn said.

"If we sit together at lunch, we could just pass it under the table," Anna suggested.

It was quiet for a minute while we all considered this possibility. It was a big deal and not a big deal at the same time.

"Let's do it," Robbie said.

"And I could tell you guys what to say in the messages," Anna added.

"Yeah," Cat said. "And we should only send a couple a night. Just enough to be intriguing and annoying but not like psycho."

"Oh, she's going to go psycho, all right," Anna said, grinning. "I'll bring you guys a list tomorrow. And then we'll let Operation Mother Stalker get started."

"No offense," Robbie said, "but that sounds like a really weird—and not in a good way—horror movie."

"Perfect," Anna said. Then she reached behind her. "This is for you, Lucas," she said. I gulped. My mason jar was full, practically overflowing with acorn caps. "We all pitched in while you were gone."

"Yeah, you always helped us," Cat said.

"Oh," I said. The boards of the fort creaked as I leaned forward to take the jar. "Thanks." Even though it was the opposite of how I felt. "Well, we have to do your thing first," I said weakly.

Anna blinked. She looked a little confused. Maybe she expected me to be happier, so I tried to smile. "But, um, thanks."

CHAPTER 23

THE NEXT DAY I WALKED INTO SCIENCE CLASS A FEW
minutes early and went right to the shelf with the bones
and shells on it. "Order and storm," Ms. Edgerly said
without even looking up from her desk. "That's what he
used to say." I turned it over from the dark swirly side to
the neat lines on the other side. I nodded. That's what
it was. It reminded me again of what Mom used to say
about people's outsides and their insides. I wondered if
Charlie had ever felt that way.

As the other kids started to drift in, I went to my seat,
keeping the shell in the palm of my hand. At the end of
class, I slipped it back on the shelf before leaving.

Anna came to the fort that afternoon with a list of

things we were supposed to text her mom over the next five nights.

Pay attention
Why don't you see me?
The best things in life aren't things
Wake up already
I miss you
I'm right in front of you (we debated for a while about
    whether or not this one was too risky)
One day I'll be gone
Do you even know what you're missing?
You'll miss me when I'm gone
Your life is not an app

We ripped the paper into more or less equal pieces and each of us memorized our assigned phrases before tearing them into little bits and sprinkling them into the snow around the fort. Finn agreed to take the phone for the first night.

The next morning, when I saw Anna in English class, she gave me a smile and a little thumbs-up. At lunch I sat down at my usual table. I was about to dig into the school lasagna, something Robbie and I called the noodle log, when Anna came over and sat down with her purple flowered lunch bag. She was sitting sideways in the chair like she wasn't sure if she belonged.

"Lucas, it was amazing!" she said.

Cory Kepperman, who usually sat with us, came walking over with his tray. When he saw Anna sitting there, his eyes widened and he quickly turned away, like Superman from kryptonite, to find another table. Anna looked up confused. "Am I in his seat?"

"No, he probably just thinks he's in the wrong place. Or maybe he's scared."

"I'm not scary," Anna said.

"Well, you are a girl. . . ."

Anna's eyebrows leaned in toward her nose as she watched Cory Kepperman scurry away toward a table in the far corner of the lunchroom. Then, slowly, she swung her legs under the table and gently placed her lunch bag on top. "Well, is it okay with *you* if I sit here? I mean, I thought that was the plan."

"Sure," I said.

"I just didn't want to wait until this afternoon to tell you guys about, you know, the phone thing." She looked around the lunchroom as if she were seeing it for the first time. "This is a cool table."

"It's okay."

"Where's Finn?" Anna asked.

"He passed me the phone in math so he could eat lunch in the library. He told me he likes to read the newspaper and do the crossword."

Anna laughed and shook her head. Out of the corner of my eye I saw Cat looking at us from over at her table of basketball girls. She waited until the lunch monitor's back was turned and then booked it over to us, sliding into a seat without being detected.

Robbie was the only one of the regulars who sat down with us. He looked perplexed. "Where is everyone else?" he asked.

I shrugged. "Scared of a girl."

"I brought my cube so I could show Kepperman how to solve it." He placed a weird-looking Rubik's Cube on the lunch table. The sides were hexagon-shaped, with gold and silver pieces.

"So," he said, looking at Anna, "did your mom go crazy last night or what?"

"Oh yeah," Anna said. She pulled a Tupperware out of

her lunch bag, opened it, and then opened another small container of salad dressing, which she spread over the salad inside.

"What is that?" Robbie asked.

"My lunch."

"I'm sorry about that," Robbie said.

Anna shrugged. "I like salad."

"Girls are weird," he concluded, taking a huge bite of his noodle log. I didn't tell him about the glop of tomato sauce on his chin, and he didn't seem to notice or care.

"Anyway," Anna said, turning toward me, "it was perfect. Finn sent the texts right at six thirty like he said he would. I was so nervous I kept doing and redoing the same math problem because I couldn't focus on anything else. I couldn't even tell if she was getting them, though, 'cause she's always on her phone, so it never pings or beeps or anything. But all of a sudden she started making these weird noises, like 'Huh?' and saying, 'What on earth?' Then she came over and picked up my phone. I made sure it was sitting right in front of me too. I even pretended to get annoyed and asked her what she was doing."

"What did she say?" I asked.

"She said it was nothing. And then she got on my case about going over our data plan. Like that's really my fault."

Just then Nicole walked by our table. She gave Anna a long, serious look and then walked away. Anna pretended she didn't notice, but it would have been pretty hard not to. "Anyway, I can't wait for tonight. Whose turn is it?"

"Mine," I said, holding up the phone and then quickly sliding it back into my pocket. I had already planned my excuse for leaving the house and going outside. It was trash day, and I usually helped Mr. Boudreau with bringing in all the trash and recycle bins. If Dad asked me where I was going, that was what I'd say.

That night after I helped Mr. Boudreau, I stood underneath one of the streetlamps that lit the lane between the rows of trailers with a soft pinkish glow. Snow was falling, but it was featherlight and there was no wind. I took the cell phone out from my jeans pocket, where I'd kept it hidden all day, and selected the number that had been saved since last night. I tapped in the phrases I'd been assigned. And then, just in case the signal from the phone might follow me inside, I waited a few minutes, imagining the texts traveling on some gust of cold night air from my hand to the inside of Anna's house, where I pictured a fake fire flickering in the gas fireplace and music that was just different enough to be cool playing on a sound system.

I wondered if Anna was as nervous as she had been the first night and if she thought at all about me standing in the cold sending the messages. I went back inside and buried the phone under my pillow. Having the phone in my house made me feel a little less lonely. There was someone on the other side of it who might, in just a teeny-tiny way, be thinking of me.

CHAPTER 24

I WOKE UP EARLY THE NEXT MORNING TO CRASHING AND clattering sounds coming from the kitchen. When I dragged myself out of bed, I found Dad standing in a pile of what looked like all the pots and pans we owned, a bottle of cleaning spray in one hand and a roll of paper towels tucked under his arm. "This place could use some sprucing up," he said.

I looked at the clock. It was half an hour before I actually had to get up to make my bus. "You never noticed before."

He scowled. "You know, Lucas, sometimes you might want things to change but not know where to start." I was so surprised that I didn't know how to respond, but it didn't really matter, since he went back to spraying some spaghetti sauce that had been glued to the cabinet door for so long it had turned from red to brown. I stared at his back, trying to work up the courage to ask him what else he wanted to change, but before I could put it in words he said, "You can put these dishes away after school."

I thought of a lot of things I could say back, but nothing that wouldn't get me more cleaning chores. When I got out of the shower, Dad was gone, and I was glad I hadn't back-talked him more. There were dishes all over the countertops just waiting for when I got home from school. I put some stuff away before the bus came, but I was rushing, and I managed to pinch my finger in one of the cabinet door hinges so hard it produced a shiny blood blister and a bad mood that lasted all the way to school.

Before I left, I took the phone out from under my pillow, wrapped it in some gym socks, and stuffed it into my bag. In the bottom of my backpack my fingers grazed the empty beer bottle I had hidden there and completely forgotten about. When I got to school, I took advantage of the pre-homeroom crush to pull the bottle from my bag and shove it in the back of my locker. My hands were so sweaty I was afraid the glass was going to slip through my fingers and shatter on the floor. I figured I'd wait until the end of the day and then find a trash can where I could stuff it in the bottom and be done with the whole thing.

I slammed my locker closed and caught sight of Finn in the hallway. I quickened my pace to catch up to him as he rounded a corner. "Finn!"

He turned around, and a small paper fluttered out of his hand. A flash of panic flew across his usually calm face as I leaned down to grab it.

It was a fortune, like the kind that came in takeout Chinese cookies. It was creased and folded down the middle like it had been pressed into a wallet for a long time. "You dropped this." Even as I spoke, my thumb found the crease and opened it up. It said, *You will be rewarded for your kindness to others.* Kids pushed past us, rushing toward homeroom. But we stood there like two rocks in a stream with a swirling eddy between us. Finn's cheeks turned pink. "It's not my sole motivation," he said.

"It's okay." I thought for a moment about how Finn didn't have an acorn jar of his own. "What do you want? For your reward?"

"A family," he said simply. The bell rang, and the hallway quickly drained of kids; classroom doors slammed around us. We would be late to homeroom, but I didn't care. Listening seemed like the least I could do.

"What about the people you live with now?"

"Kind enough, but not family." I contemplated this and thought about my own situation. As if he could read my mind, Finn said, "And your father?"

"Family, but not very kind."

"Perhaps in time . . ."

Words filled up in my chest like hot lava. Before I could stop myself, they spewed out of my mouth. "I don't get it! Why do some people get both? Why do some people get good families with parents who actually want them around, who don't just treat them like the leftovers? Why do some people stay together and love each other, and some people just drift apart and don't care at all about how they treat everyone?" My face felt hot, and I wondered for a second if I was really going to throw up all over the place.

Finn appeared unfazed by my outburst. "Certainly unfair. Apparently unavoidable, it would seem." He smiled weakly. "There's always this, though."

"What?"

"Friends."

"Yeah, friends." I handed him the little fortune, which he creased and placed carefully back in his pocket.

Anna was nowhere to be seen at lunch. I worried I had done something wrong and that her mom had figured the whole thing out. But when I saw her in between classes she told me that she had eaten lunch in art class so she could finish a project that was due. Her eyes were sparkling when she grabbed my arm and said, "You're not going to believe what my mom did." She glanced around for a second, but the hall was full of kids and the bell was about to ring. "I'll tell you all about it later."

That afternoon we went out to the fort even though it was freezing cold. When the temperature dropped below thirty, Steve wasn't supposed to let us go. It was above the mark, but with the wind, I winced every time a gust blew through the tree fort and found the places where last year's jacket didn't quite meet the waistband of my pants.

Once we moved enough snow off the platform to sit, we huddled together to stay warm. Anna cleared her throat and said, "You guys, it worked."

"What do you mean?" Cat asked.

"Last night my mom sat down at the table where I was doing my homework and asked if I thought she worked too much. She wanted to know if she spent enough time with me!" Anna was beaming.

"What did you say?" Cat asked.

"I told her I felt like she ignored me, and she was always staring at her stupid phone! I thought she was going to yell at me, but you know what she said? She said she thought all teenagers wanted their space."

"You're in sixth grade," Robbie said. "That's not even officially a teenager."

"I know, right? Then she totally started in on the excuses. There was that one, and how her job is so stressful and the pressure she feels to be perfect because she's a Black woman."

My eyes got wide. I wasn't sure what any of us were supposed to say. I looked down. Besides Anna there was only one other Black kid in our grade. Anna never talked about that with us. Maybe she felt like she couldn't. I had never talked to anyone about what color their skin was before, I guess because I'd never had to. I hoped that wasn't a racist thing to think. How would I know if it was?

"But you're her kid" slipped out of my mouth.

Anna looked at me straight on. "That's what I told her. She actually started to cry, even though I told her I didn't need her to be perfect either.

"Anyway, she made this schedule. Which, by the way, is *so my mom*. Supposedly she's going to be 'device free' from the time we get home until eight o'clock every night. She said that's going to be *our* time. Like if I need help on my homework, or we can watch a show together or paint our toenails. Whatever I want," Anna said proudly. "She even bought this cute box with sparkles on it and stuff. She said that's where the phone goes until eight. I totally think she read that on a parenting website. I was using her iPad and there were all these tabs open about reconnecting with your teen." She shook her head. "That's Mom—gotta research everything and do it the right way." Anna's voice was sarcastic but happy. Her eyes were happy. She shook some of the snow off the branch behind her and molded it into a tiny ball, which she threw directly at me.

"So that means it's your turn, Lucas Barnes!"

I'd had plenty of time to think of a wish—a fake wish. The things I really wanted I was sure were beyond the power of any acorn caps to grant. I wanted my family back. My mouth went dry. I opened and closed it a few times like a fish gasping on land.

Then, intentionally or not, Robbie saved me. "What are we going to do with the phone?"

I pulled it out of my coat pocket and placed it on a spot of dry wood. Robbie said, "My little brother Marcus is pretty good with technology. He could probably wipe all the data for us. You know, in case anybody ever found it."

Nobody said anything, so Cat pushed the phone toward Robbie.

"Operation Superwipe!" he said excitedly.

"Ew," said Cat and Anna together.

"Yeah, I'll work on that," Robbie said.

"What are you going to do with it once he, um, wipes it?" Cat asked.

"I'll smash it," Robbie said. "Or bury it in the woods."

"Yes," said Finn. "Obliterate the evidence."

I nodded too, but I was still looking down. I could feel Anna's eyes on me. She knew I had avoided her question. She still wanted to know about my wish. A million different scenarios ran through my mind. I could jump down from the tree and run away from there as fast as possible. I could tell them all to leave me alone. I could tell them I'd never had a wish, that I thought the whole thing was stupid. But then it would all be over. I was the only one left playing the game. If I didn't have a wish to work on, then what were we all doing there? Maybe we wouldn't even come outside anymore, and things would just go back to the way they had been. I didn't want that. I didn't want my friends to go away.

"I want my mom back." I looked away, up into the thick branches of the pine tree above us. I half expected them all to start laughing at me. When I dared to look back down, I saw something I didn't expect. Anna was nodding her head.

"Yes," she said. "This will be our biggest challenge yet."

Robbie clapped a hand on my knee.

"We should go in," Cat said. "We're going to need the internet."

CHAPTER 25

STEVE DIDN'T SEEM TO NOTICE OR CARE WHEN WE ALL came in early from outside time, or when we all gave him a variety of ridiculous excuses for why we had to go back into the main part of the building in order to secretly meet up at the library.

Cat and I ran through the hallways like secret agents, ducking beneath the windows when we saw a custodian cleaning out a classroom. My heart was pounding in my chest as my mind scrambled around trying to figure out how much and what to tell my friends.

It was Friday afternoon so the library was empty and dark, but the door was open. There was one reference computer still on, an internet browser window open and Google shining brightly into the world like an invitation to find out everything you possibly could, but nothing you actually needed to know. Robbie slid into the chair and turned to look at me. "What should I type?"

I had that hot feeling in my chest again. "Alexandra Barnes," I whispered. I watched as Robbie typed the letters in one at a time and pressed the button to search.

I don't know what I expected. If it was going to be this easy, I could have simply searched for her myself. But of course there were thousands, if not millions, of Alexandra Barneses. My heart sank as the pages and pages of entries stacked up: little blue lines to click on and find other Alexandra Barneses. Robbie switched the search to images, but none of them looked like Mom.

"We need more search parameters," he said. "Do you have any idea where she might be? Like what part of the country?"

"Western Massachusetts," I said. "That's where my aunt Sheila lives. Maybe in a hospital?" My voice cracked on this last part. Robbie's hands hovered over the keyboard. The click of a door handle broke the silence.

"Are you kids supposed to be in here?" It was the female

custodian. I didn't know her name, but she always had music playing as she pushed her trash can decorated with stuffed animal Beanie Babies through the hallways. We all jumped back from the screen.

"We have a pass," Finn said, holding up a yellow sticky note with something scribbled on it.

The custodian's eyes flicked between our faces and the yellow scrap in Finn's hand. "You kids are from that Teen Club in the cafeteria?"

We nodded.

"You're not supposed to be in here this late. You tell that to whoever's in charge down there. Go on and get back now. I gotta clean up."

We practically exploded out the library doors into the hallway, all talking at the same time about our run-in with the law. We made a plan to sneak back to the library on Monday, but my stomach was twisting in knots. How much would I have to tell them? How much did I even really know? To them it was like a crime show or a missing-person case. But Mom wasn't exactly lost. She was exactly where she wanted to be, and nothing we were doing was going to change that part.

Before we could resume our mission-impossible activities, something happened that none of us saw coming. On Monday Anna's mother showed up at school. I signed out to go to the bathroom about ten minutes before class ended, which was always a good way to kill those last few minutes before lunch. The closest bathroom was locked, so I turned the corner to go down to the next one, and that's when I saw her standing at the end of the hall outside the entrance to the front office.

She was tapping her foot and staring down at her phone. She did not look happy. I didn't know why she was there, but I got a cold, sweaty feeling on the back of my neck. I didn't have to go to the bathroom anymore. I whipped around and walked quickly back to class.

When I got to lunch, both Anna and Cat were already sitting at our table. Anna looked mad. "Why did you text my mom and tell her she has a nice butt?"

Robbie and I both froze, lunch trays in hand. Slowly I turned my head to look at him. His face was on fire. Neither of us spoke.

"Sit down," Anna whispered. "People are staring."

We slid our trays onto the table and sat opposite the girls like we were on trial. "I—I didn't," Robbie stammered.

"Well then, who?" Anna said.

Robbie squirmed in his seat. "I gave it to Marcus on Friday to wipe the data. I had to give him all the rest of my birthday money to do it. He probably thought I was texting a girl or something and did it to be funny. I'm going to kill him!"

"Evil genius," I said darkly.

"Well, my mom is here and she's wicked mad. I don't know what she's going to do."

After lunch we found out. The classroom phone rang while Ms. Edgerly was trying to get us interested in the arrangement of the periodic table. "Sure," she said, "I'll send them down." Her eyes flickered with amusement when she called out, "Finn, Lucas, you're wanted down in the office."

As we walked toward the door, Robbie stared at us wide-eyed and Sadie Gillespie whispered, "What did you do?"

Finn whispered back, "Ecoterrorism." Sadie squinted at him.

"What's that?" I asked when we got in the hall.

"Something interesting for her to spread around."

"Aren't you worried?" I asked.

"Not especially. I can't think of a single way they could link that phone to anyone but Robbie. Just pretend like you have no idea what we're doing there."

"Do you do this a lot? I mean before, at your old school. Did you get in trouble a lot?"

"Not exactly," Finn answered cryptically. "Let's just say I have some experience dealing with adults in difficult situations."

CHAPTER 26

MR. COUGHLIN WAS STANDING OUTSIDE THE OFFICE WHEN we got there. He looked very agitated and kept pulling on his tie and cracking his knuckles. Mrs. Perkins was standing right behind him, glaring at us. "Gentlemen," he said, "this is Mrs. Perkins. She's the mother of one of your classmates. And"—he paused and coughed into his hand—"she has received some unusual text messages lately. And, well, she seems to think that it's coming from a friend of Anna's, someone here at school."

"Someone from that after-school program." Mrs. Perkins spoke over his shoulder. She had a piercing look that made me feel guilty even though I wasn't—at least not of

198

telling her she had a nice butt.

Mr. Coughlin looked at us like he was expecting us to make the next move. But I had no idea what that was, and apparently neither did Finn. Finally, Mrs. Perkins coughed loudly, so I said, "I don't have a cell phone."

"Neither do I," said Finn, maybe a tad too cheerfully.

"Well, then," Mr. Coughlin said to Mrs. Perkins. "There you have it."

"That's *it*? That's all you're going to do? You can send text messages without a phone, you know! They have all kinds of ways on iPad and iTouch and whatever else. I'm telling you, *these* are the kids. There's more of them too. She has to hang out with them because of that after-school program you claim to be running here. Did you know that they are going outside unsupervised? I'm telling you who the kids are, and all you're going to do is ask them if they have a cell phone? You're not even going to search their lockers?"

This was definitely not the part we were supposed to be hearing, so I took a tiny step backward to give the appearance of not listening to the entire adult conversation.

Mr. Coughlin fumbled with his tie some more and looked nervously down the hall in either direction. Maybe he was hoping for a burst pipe or a fight to break up, something that would pull him away from the angry parent and her accused.

"Well, um, I don't really think we have enough information to justify a locker search at this time," he said. "The boys have rights, you know."

"Not at school we don't," Finn said.

My jaw dropped.

"We have no expected right to privacy or protection against search and seizure in school," he explained. "It's in the school handbook."

Mrs. Perkins's eyebrows were up around her hairline. Mr. Coughlin looked annoyed, and I was about to whack Finn upside the head. Was he nuts? What was he trying to do?

"Are there any cell phones in your lockers?" Mr. Coughlin said. He sounded very tired.

"Not that I know of," Finn answered. I just shook my head.

Mr. Coughlin looked hopefully back at Mrs. Perkins, who was scowling at him. "I suppose I'll have to get the school resource officer for this. But you'll have to wait in the office. I can't have parents be a part of something like this." He stood up a little taller and said, "That would be inappropriate."

Mrs. Perkins disappeared into the office, and Officer Bob appeared a few minutes later, bouncing on his toes. Feltzer Harding Middle School probably didn't have a lot of unsolved mysteries. "All right, boys, let's go check out these lockers," he said excitedly, pointing with his foot-long black flashlight in the direction of the sixth-grade hallway.

We got to my locker first. I opened it up and a sheaf of math worksheets fell out onto the hallway floor. My textbooks were battered, with brown-paper book covers hanging off at the corners, and my three-ring binders were crammed in at different angles. My coat, hat, and smelly gym bag were stuffed in at the top. I started pulling everything out, but when I got to the second layer of books and binders, Mr. Coughlin just waved his hand and told me to stuff it all back in. Then something clanked.

"What's that?" Officer Bob asked, flicking on his flashlight and temporarily blinding me. Officer Bob pushed past me and pulled from the back of my locker the empty beer bottle I had hidden there. I remembered the plan I had made to wait until after school and ditch it in the trash can while the hallways were empty. But I hadn't. Clearly, I hadn't. I glanced desperately at Finn.

"This is a problem, young man," Mr. Coughlin said.

I felt sick. My face went hot, and my feet went cold and clammy all at the same time. They were going to have to call Dad. I didn't even care if he got mad about the beer bottle. I just knew how furious he'd be to have to miss work because I screwed up. "It's not a cell phone," I pointed out weakly.

"I have some too!" Finn said brightly.

I ogled him. Mr. Coughlin scratched his head. Only Officer Bob didn't find this to be a strange confession. "Where's *your* locker, son?" he said in an ultra-serious voice.

Finn strutted off down the hallway like a happy peacock. I had no idea what he was doing or thinking. I was still clutching the beer bottle in my sweaty hand. I looked desperately at the trash can as we passed it thinking maybe I could toss it in and nobody would be the wiser.

In Finn's locker each textbook was lined up carefully next to the others, spines covered neatly with perfectly folded brown-paper book covers labeled in exceptionally neat handwriting. A single spiral notebook leaned up against a single three-ring binder. His vest hung on the metal hook. Miraculously, Finn reached behind the coat and pulled out a plastic bag that was bulging and clinked like glass on glass.

"See," he said, "I've got some too!"

"Those are beer bottles?" Mr. Coughlin asked.

Finn stared down into the bag. "Well, some of them probably are." He reached in just as one of the plastic handles snapped, sending the contents of the bag spilling and clanking out across the green and white tile floor. The smell of old dirt and stagnant water filled the air.

"Ugh," said Mr. Coughlin. "What *is* all this?"

"Well, Lucas and I and some of the other kids—we found this old junk pile in the woods. We've been cleaning it up out there. We were worried about younger kids finding it and getting cut on the glass. We found some older bottles too and we thought they might be worth something. We keep the stuff in our lockers so we can look it up online or recycle it when we get home. You know, Mr. Coughlin," Finn said, wide-eyed and serious, "the school could really benefit from a more comprehensive recycling plan."

"Boys!" Mr. Coughlin cut him off with a hand held up in the air. "THIS. IS. NOT. EARTH. DAY."

"I thought we were supposed to treat every day like Earth Day," Finn said quietly.

My jaw dropped again. But Finn's face was perfect: perfectly serious and perfectly sincere.

Now Officer Bob looked annoyed. "I don't really see any legal issues here, Pete. The kids were cleaning up the woods."

Mr. Coughlin looked at his watch. "Clean up this mess," he barked at us. "Bring the trash to my office so I can figure out what to do with it. I'll deal with Mrs. Perkins later."

Finn and I gathered up the bottles as quickly as possible. I was so relieved to have a task that didn't involve leaving in handcuffs, I couldn't move fast enough. When we were done cleaning up the bottles and mopping the floor with about a hundred of the wimpy paper towels from the bathroom, we looked up at each other. The front of Finn's hair flopped forward, and the knees of his khaki pants were wet from the floor. I couldn't help it. I busted up laughing. My belly ached. It was so ridiculous, the two of us mopping up like the world's most inept underage custodians. Finn was laughing too—real laughter that made him look and sound more like a kid than he ever had before.

We went back to class and collected our things. Finn had French and I didn't. We paused in the hallway, where he would go one way and I would go another. Then we stood there awkwardly. He must have realized the beer bottle hadn't come from the woods. But he didn't ask, and I didn't offer.

"Thanks," I said.

"Not a problem."

"How come you're so good at lying?" I meant it to sound appreciative, but maybe it didn't.

Finn just shrugged. *"Perfectus usus facit."*

"Practice makes perfect?" I guessed.

Finn executed a little bow, turned neatly on his heel, and proceeded down the hall.

CHAPTER 27

I WAS JUMPY THE REST OF THE DAY. WHENEVER THE
bell rang, or even when someone screeched their chair
backward against the tile floor, my head shot around like
an owl. When we got to Teen Club that afternoon, Robbie
and Cat shared their own experiences being interrogated
by Mr. Coughlin and Anna's mom. I guess Mr. Coughlin
had been a little scarred by the experience with me and
Finn, because he took their word for it when they told him
they didn't have cell phones.

Steve let us go to the library after we invented a very
complicated group project that required research, but our
afternoon session there was cut short by Mr. Flanagan, who
kept hovering around us and offering unhelpful search tips

that seemed like they came from the year the internet was invented. After twenty minutes he asked us to leave because the library was reserved for a school-board committee meeting. Anna offered to use her phone, but her service wasn't great inside school. Everyone promised to use their home computers to keep looking, but I was feeling more embarrassed than optimistic. What kind of a person loses their mother?

By the time Dad picked me up that afternoon, I was worn out from the constant adrenaline pumping through my veins. Once we pulled away from school, I slumped down in my seat. The heat was on full blast in Dad's truck, and even though the classic-rock station was blaring some annoying song about the good old days, my eyelids started to feel heavy and my body felt like a sack of sand.

Dad stopped at the entrance to Oak Hill, left the motor running, and jumped out of the truck. I saw him grab some beer from the back and run it into Mr. Boudreau's trailer. When he came back out, he was empty-handed.

"Early Christmas present?"

"Needed to get rid of it," Dad mumbled.

"Why?"

Dad patted his middle. "I don't need it around the house right now."

"Oh."

"During the week. I could probably lay off during the week. Metabolism slows down when you hit forty anyway." I pulled nervously at the front of my shirt, waiting for him to make a comment about me or my lack of athletic ability, but he didn't say anything else.

I had never ever seen Dad give away beer except on Christmas, but I was too tired to figure out what to make of this new development. I watched TV and went to bed without doing my homework.

"Finn's not here," Anna said the next day at lunch when she sat down and began to unpack her food. Cat was there too.

"Maybe he's sick," Robbie said.

Anna shrugged. "He left early out of social studies. Like right away as soon as class started, he got called down, and Mrs. McCafferty looked kind of weird and sad when someone asked if they should put work in the absent folder for Finn. Like she hesitated."

"He was here *this morning*," I said.

"I don't know. It was weird the way she hesitated, like he might not be back for a while."

I got up and walked over to the lunch monitor to get a bathroom pass. I walked straight past the bathrooms to the hallway where Finn's locker was. I remembered that the greenish stain forming at the base of the wall next to his locker looked like the shape of a deflated heart. I jiggled the handle, but like all Feltzer Harding lockers it had a combination lock built in. Sometimes kids jammed theirs open with a pencil, but it didn't surprise me that Finn wasn't one of them. I pressed my face against the slats at the top of the locker, trying to get a glimpse inside. I was relieved to see that it was unchanged from yesterday, except for his absent jacket.

The rest of the day was more boring, less shiny, without Finn there to make some random World War II reference that no one else, sometimes even the teacher, knew about, or to solve a problem in math at the board calling all the numbers "ladies or gents," as he sometimes did.

After school we walked half-heartedly out to the fort and sat there without saying much. Robbie started throwing out some random theories, like maybe Finn had been abducted by aliens or was in the witness protection program, but I was only half listening. I could see into the future: all of us drifting apart going back to our old lunch tables and maybe just saying hi when we passed in the halls and then one day not at all. Maybe I wasn't the hub at all, like Anna had said. Finn was the one who had made things different. He was the one who invented the game that actually changed things.

We sat cross-legged on the wooden boards. We were supposed to be working on my problem, but I wasn't going to bring it up if nobody else did. Robbie said he'd found an Alexandra Barnes who was a cheese maker in New York somewhere, and another one who did a circus act for weddings and kids' birthday parties. No one else had any leads at all. I was worried that without Finn we would lose momentum and my wish would fizzle out, along with any hopes I had of ever getting Mom back.

"You guys," Anna said. She paused dramatically and waited until we were all looking at her. "I pooped my pants once."

We were silent. Finally, Robbie broke the silence. "Like when you were little?"

Anna shook her head. "Last year, after gym. I thought it was just a fart, but then, you know, it wasn't."

Robbie started shaking with laughter. "That's amazing," he said. Then Anna started laughing, nervously at first. I covered my mouth with my hand and then just cracked up openly.

"What did you do?" Cat asked.

"I had to go back and put my gym clothes back on. I threw my jeans and underwear in the trash and lied to my mom about what happened to them."

"Did anyone ever find out?" Robbie asked.

"Nope," Anna said. "I mean, it's so gross, right?"

"Why are you telling us now?" Robbie asked.

"I don't know," Anna said.

But I knew, even though I wasn't sure I could explain it. Anna was worried about the same thing I was: what would happen without Finn. "I miss my mom," I said. It felt so good, I said it again. "I really miss my mom and I'm afraid I might hate my dad."

"Parents," Anna said with a big sigh, "they don't understand anything."

"I've never met my dad," Robbie said. "My dad—I mean, I call him my dad because he's the only dad I've ever known. But he's really just the little kids' dad. My mom feels bad about it, I can tell, but she never talks about it with me. I can just feel it, the way she looks at me sometimes. It's like she thinks she's depriving me of something. And then I start to wonder if she's right. Like, am I screwed up for life because I don't know this person who's actually responsible for half my DNA? I mean, Nick is a great dad. I love him."

Robbie's voice cracked and his eyes teared up. He dropped his head down and made little snuffling noises into his jacket.

"I think we're all screwed up for life," I said quietly.

Anna snort-laughed. I *had* sort of meant it to be funny.

"My mom, my dad." I rolled my eyes. "Your dad." I looked at Robbie. I looked at Anna and my mouth twitched. "Your, um, unfortunate poop situation . . ." We all started laughing again, even Anna. "I mean, everyone's got something."

It sounded obvious, but I didn't think I'd ever really known it like I knew it now.

Next to me Cat was drumming her fingers nervously against one of the wooden boards. "I don't think I like boys. I mean, I like you guys"—she chin-pointed at me and Robbie—"but I don't *like* like you, or any of you."

"Whoa," said Anna. "Do you, um, like girls?"

Cat shrugged. "I don't know. Maybe? It's just like crushes on boys and stuff people talk about, I don't have any of that. Even when I'm with my friends on the team, I feel different, and I don't think I could ever tell them about it. So then I'm just different and alone."

"You're not alone," I said. But was I talking to Cat or telling myself?

"Yeah," Anna said. "It's cool, whoever you like or don't like."

The air was cold, but I felt warm and nervous too. How did Cat know that? I guess she knew the same way I knew that when Anna talked to me, my palms got all sweaty.

"Wow," Anna said. "Well, there *is* one more secret."

"I don't know if I can take any more secrets," Robbie said.

"We need to find out what's going on with Finn," Anna said, with steely determination.

CHAPTER 28

FINN WASN'T IN SCHOOL THE NEXT DAY EITHER, AND THEN we had the long weekend for Thanksgiving. Mrs. Boudreau invited me and Dad over, which made a lonely thing a little less lonely. She sent us home with a ton of leftovers, which was awesome. When I wasn't eating leftover turkey sandwiches and watching the Bruins with Dad, I caught up on some homework and tried to build a replica of the Death Star with Dad's old space Legos.

When we got back on Monday there was still no Finn. We asked Steve for his contact information, but Steve said it was a legal thing and he couldn't give it out without permission. We tried his school email, but most kids never looked at that anyway. So there was nothing. A big white space on a wall where a crazy colorful piece of art had been. I packed up slowly at the end of the day. On my way to Teen Club I took a turn and walked slowly past the science room. Ms. Edgerly was sitting at her desk in front of a large pile of tests and quizzes. I walked over to the shelf with the nature stuff on it and picked up my favorite shell. I flipped it over in my hand a few times. Order and storm. Ms. Edgerly looked up and squinted at me. "What's going on, Lucas?"

"Where did Finn go?"

She put down the paper she was holding and sighed. "You're asking about our friend Mr. Clark?"

I nodded.

"He'll be back." Her eyes flicked off to the side when she said it. She didn't even try to lie and say he was sick.

"Why didn't he say anything? Did he know he was leaving?"

She sighed. "I'm sorry. I really can't . . . I mean, I'm not allowed to say more. Kids in Finn's . . . situation experience a lot of uncertainty. It's not ideal, but he's probably used to it."

I scowled. Such a typical adult answer. Just assume the kid can deal with some crappy situation because he's had to deal with it before. Ms. Edgerly looked right at me and said rather curtly, "I'm sorry. I know it's not the answer you were looking for." She looked back down at the papers she was grading. I knew it was supposed to be my cue to leave.

"Why don't you like me?" I blurted out. Before she could answer, I said, "You were my brother's favorite teacher. And I thought—" I stopped, unsure of what I did think. "I thought you would be different."

Ms. Edgerly looked up from the stack of student work. She cocked her head to the side and looked at me with a weird expression and a twisted-up mouth. "I'm sorry you think that. I don't . . . I don't *not* like you. It's complicated."

"Whatever," I said. "Everyone always liked Charlie better anyway. The better student, better at sports, popular, all that."

Ms. Edgerly let out a loud, short laugh. Of all the responses I'd thought I would get, laughter was not one of them. "Is that what you really think? You think I don't like you because you're not Charlie? Is that what it's really like for you?"

I stared at her. "Yeah, it is."

"Your brother was a real pain, Lucas!"

I stared back. Was she making fun of me?

"He was not a very good student, either—whatever that even means. The kids liked him. Okay, they loved him. And I loved him. That's not something teachers say a lot.

I guess we're not supposed to say we love our students, but we do. Not all of them, of course. But we do. Have you ever talked about Charlie to your teachers who had him? I mean, really talked to them?"

"I don't know," I said.

"Well, he was a piece of work. In his seat, out of his seat, always blurting out. He was smart, that's true. But he was *not* a typical good student." She said this last bit with air quotes. "His work was always sloppy, disorganized, sometimes days late." She paused and rested her cheek on her fist. "But he was such a good kid. He cared about learning. He got excited about science, the same way you do."

I blushed. No one ever said I was like Charlie.

"I see it in your answers." She held up a few of our quizzes, the ones we'd taken just last week on the parts of an atom. "You remember little things, like the size of the empty space inside an atom."

A weird, warm feeling washed over me.

"But you hide, Lucas. It's not so easy to get to know you. Everything about Charlie was out there: loud, exuberant, fun-loving. Of course his teachers remember him. You don't have to be like Charlie, but you don't have to hide yourself either. You're a person worth knowing all on your own, no matter who your brother was."

I pressed the edge of the shell into my hand, considering her words and everything they might mean.

"Charlie was on honor roll. He got all those awards," I said.

"I didn't say he wasn't smart. Charlie was very smart, but he also had a lot of challenges. Do you know what ADHD is? Attention deficit hyperactivity disorder?"

"Kind of." A kid in my class last year had talked about having it. He was always bouncing his leg and making the table jiggle.

"Well," she said carefully, "I think—no, I know—Charlie had a kind of ADHD." She paused as though deciding whether or not to proceed. "I thought he should be tested. I spoke with your parents about it. But, well . . ." She sighed. "He was doing okay in school. They didn't see what I saw in the classroom: how hard he had to work to appear like everyone else, to get the grades he was getting."

"But Charlie didn't act . . . I don't know . . . I know this is wrong, but he didn't seem, you know, hyper or whatever."

"It's called 'inattentive type.' It means you have trouble focusing, but you show it by losing track of time, staring out the window, spacing out. Does that sound more like Charlie?"

"I guess so." What I didn't say was that it really sounded like Mom.

"How old were you when Charlie was in sixth grade?"

"Uh, three."

She gave me a sad look. "Midway through sixth grade his grades started to slip. The work was getting harder, and he was struggling to keep up. When your parents wouldn't agree to the testing, I started to tutor him. Charlie stayed after school with me most days through the end of eighth grade. Even in high school he still came down when he needed help writing an essay or if he had a particularly tough chemistry test."

I made a face. I remembered Charlie complaining about chemistry. "No wonder he liked you so much."

"Charlie was great," Ms. Edgerly said. "But here's the thing, Lucas. I was probably too involved."

"Why? Because you cared about him?"

"No, because I made his success my success. It shouldn't have been about me. I should have helped him reach out more at the high school. I should have helped him advocate for himself. No one was prouder of Charlie when he got that scholarship to UMaine. But I should have known it would be a rough transition—all those new classes and teachers, and the reading alone would have been more than he could handle. I think Charlie was in over his head at college and, well, I think he got desperate. I think he might have tried to self-medicate, maybe to help him focus at first, but then . . ." She let the sentence hang.

My eyebrows knit together as I stared at her. Ms. Edgerly waited a second as if she expected me to say something, or to know something, but I didn't.

"Teachers aren't supposed to save people, Lucas. Not the good ones, anyway. They're supposed to help you realize your own . . . your own . . . I don't know how to put it exactly. When your brother died"—she paused and swallowed—"I felt responsible. I felt like when I made it about myself, I let him down."

"But it was an accident; the roads were icy that night."

"I know," she said. "But he was . . . I should have . . . Anyway, the thing is, when you walked into my classroom, it just reminded me of a part of myself I've tried hard to change."

"I don't think you should change caring about people," I blurted out.

Ms. Edgerly smiled that smile adults give you when you're missing something they think they can't possibly explain. And even though she was a teacher, I rolled my eyes at her. She didn't call me on it, though; she just kept talking. "Every time I looked at you, I thought of Charlie. But now that I know you, I *do* like you. A lot, in fact. Because you're you—not because you're Charlie's brother."

"But you still can't tell me where Finn went, huh?"

Ms. Edgerly threw back her head and laughed. I liked making her laugh. "I wish I could, Lucas, but I can't. Truthfully, I don't even really know many of the details. But if I did . . ."

"You couldn't tell me." I sighed.

CHAPTER 29

MY HEAD WAS SPINNING AFTER TALKING TO MS. EDGERLY.
The stuff she'd said about Charlie was as bizarre as if she'd
pointed up at the ceiling and called it the floor. And at the
same time, I knew that what she was saying was true, or
at least part of the truth.

On my way down to the cafeteria I stopped by the
trophy case and looked carefully at the picture of Charlie
behind the glass. Eighth-grade Charlie had a big line of
angry-looking pimples across his forehead. I didn't remember
Charlie having bad skin. I guess by the time I was forming
memories, it had all cleared up. Did the truth matter now
that he was gone? It didn't change how much I loved and
missed my brother. But if Charlie had had that thing Ms.

Edgerly talked about, maybe Mom had it too? Suddenly I felt a little queasy. I turned quickly away and nearly crashed right into Anna.

"Hey," she said.

"Sorry."

"It's okay. Hey, is that your brother?" I nodded. "He looks nice," she said.

"He died," I said.

She nodded. "Robbie told me."

I was glad Anna didn't feel like she had to say anything else. We just stood there for a minute looking at Charlie. I tilted my head to one side. Charlie did look nice. He had a nice warm smile. But it was just a picture, and I wasn't so certain about the truth behind the picture. Was he Ms. Edgerly's Charlie, or Mom's Charlie, or the Charlie I thought I remembered? Maybe he was all of them, the same way Dad could be such a jerk sometimes but then could do something really nice, like make Mom that writing shack and never tell anyone about it.

Anna and I walked down to the cafeteria, and I told her what Ms. Edgerly had said about Finn. Anna sighed and shook her head. "We're his friends. We have a right to know what's going on with him." She swung her arms back and forth as she walked, and the back of her hand caught the back of mine. Our knuckles rapped together, and I felt tiny pinpricks all the way up and down my arm.

"Sorry," she said.

"It's okay."

"No, I mean I'm sorry about my mom and the other day, your locker and everything."

"Oh," I said. "Your mom is pretty intense, huh?"

Anna rolled her eyes. "You think?"

"It's okay. It was Robbie's evil little brother who messed things up. He probably has a future as a hacker or a supervillain."

"Ha!" Anna said. "You're funny, Lucas."

I smiled, trying to still look kind of cool. But Anna was already on the next topic.

After school no one else wanted to go outside. But I felt like we had to. Otherwise we were giving up on Finn and maybe each other. So after snack I stood up and said, "I'm going out."

"I've got to finish my math," Anna said quietly. Robbie and Cat just sort of looked away.

"I'm going to check on the fort," I added, but no one said anything, so I left the cafeteria and went out into the cold all alone.

The snow underneath my feet was crunchy, and the

edges of old footprints scraped my ankles through my thin socks. When I reached the fort, there was ice frozen on the wooden handholds. I was able to knock it off the lower steps, but up high I had to keep my feet carefully positioned in the middle of each step to avoid sliding off one side or the other.

Once I'd climbed up, I sat down by myself in the middle and began chipping away at some ice frozen between the boards, listening as it crackled and fell into the icy snow below. I could feel the gears of my brain turning, moving the pieces of information around and around like the colored squares on one of Robbie's Rubik's Cubes. Then I looked up. Something was missing. Finn's thermos was gone. The tin tackle box was there, and so were the jars of acorn caps, but the red plaid thermos with the olive-green top was gone. And what's more, there was a neat circle of crusty snow around bare wood where it had been sitting, probably not too long ago. Someone had been there.

CHAPTER 30

A COUPLE MORE DAYS PASSED AND THERE WAS NO SIGN
of Finn. The temperature dipped and no one wanted to go
outside. On Thursday afternoon I bundled up and went back
to the fort, but nothing else had changed since I noticed
the missing thermos. I hadn't really expected that acorn
caps would bring Mom back, but I also hadn't expected to
lose Finn. Maybe none of this worked without him. That
night I curled up in one corner of the couch and did my
math homework super slowly. I stared at the numbers. I
wrote each step out, just the way Miss LeGage did on the
board, making each line of division and multiplication line
up perfectly, pressing hard with the pencil. I just wanted to

focus on math with its rules and right or wrong answers. That's probably why it took me a while to notice that Dad was cleaning again.

More specifically, he was standing on a chair cleaning the little space that was maybe four inches between the tops of the cabinets and the ceiling. He sneezed three times in a row and followed that with some swearing. I looked around. The front of the microwave was shiny; so was the fridge. The cobweb that usually floated in the corner by the TV was also mysteriously absent.

Dad got down from the chair and wiped his face with the sleeve of his T-shirt. "Lucas," he said, "I've invited a friend to come have dinner with us on Saturday night."

"Here?"

"Yes, here."

"Who's going to cook?"

"I am." He sounded a little annoyed. "I'll clear the snow off the grill and make something."

I rolled my eyes. "It's winter."

"The grill still works in winter. You can make a salad."

"Why can't you just go out to the bar with this guy?"

Dad took a deep breath and let it out in a way that sounded somewhere between Darth Vader and a vacuum cleaner. "Well, it's not a guy, first of all. It's a girl—a woman—who . . . Well, she's a friend of mine I'd like you to meet."

"What do you mean?"

Then Dad started talking really fast. Her name was Lynn. She worked in the office. I didn't hear the rest of the details. My ears were burning and I was thinking about the name Lynn. What a stupid name. It only had one syllable. I pictured Lynn looking like this tall, awkward substitute teacher we had at school sometimes, who wore her shirts buttoned all the way up and never smiled. Mom had a beautiful name. Alexandra. It had four syllables and sounded like the name of a Greek goddess. Uh-oh—Dad was looking at me. Had he asked me a question? Was there something I was supposed to say?

"Why do you want *me* to meet her?"

"Well, we have coffee sometimes. She's a friend, like I said. And I've told her a lot about you."

"What about Mom?"

Dad's voice got really strained. "It's not like that, Lucas. But Mom's not exactly around right now, and I'm not planning to put my life on hold forever."

I snorted. It was the wrong move. Dad stood up quickly, knocking his chair over. "She's really got your number, doesn't she? You've got her on some kind of pedestal."

"What's that supposed to mean?"

"Well, in case you haven't noticed, she left *us*. And I'm the one who stuck around. I'm the one who's here."

"Wow, Dad," I said. "You're really father of the year!"

Dad's voice got low, like it did when he was going to say something mean. "You know, she didn't even fight with me about it. When I said I'd take you, she didn't say a thing, Lucas."

I bit hard on my lower lip so it wouldn't quiver. I felt the tear forming in my eye itching to roll down my nose, but I fought it. "Screw. You!" I said, and I ran past him, out the door, and past the truck. I ran until I reached the main road, and I stood there under the orange streetlight, my breath coming in short, ragged gasps. The tear that had threatened to roll down my face was now frozen against the side of my nose. Where could I go? I had nowhere to go, and there wasn't even a nearby store I could wander around until someone kicked me out. I thought briefly about running to Robbie's house but couldn't bring myself to do it. What would I say? What would Robbie's parents think?

I doubled back on the other side of the trailer park so Dad couldn't see me. I was cold. But I couldn't go crawling back into that tin box and face the fact that I was stuck with him just like he said. I could see his silhouette pacing back and forth in the main room. My mind raced for somewhere, anywhere I could go. There was the shed, but it wasn't far enough; besides, Dad would think to look for me there. I snuck around to the front where Dad's truck was parked and carefully opened the passenger side door. I grabbed his thick Carhartt coat from the seat, then took off running.

The coat was big on me, and the change in Dad's pockets banged against my thigh as I ran. I ran through the woods into Robbie's neighborhood, but I didn't stop there. Running felt good, not like in gym class where I was sure someone was watching and laughing at how slow I was. It was dark, and I felt like the night was flying by me, going a million miles an hour. The edge of the road was clear of snow, and my shoes made a satisfying slapping noise against the pavement.

I ran, my sides aching, until I ended up back at school. My feet just seemed to take me there. The parking lot was dark and empty, but there were still a few pale-yellow emergency lights on inside the building. I could easily see the path into the woods, and once I got past the first line of trees, my eyes adjusted to the darkness. I wasn't running anymore but walked quickly to the fort, afraid that I might hear noises that would make me turn around. I found the tree fort and began to climb up. I felt strong as I slammed my foot onto each wooden rung. I knew it would hold me. This was my place that I'd made with my friends.

I'd stay just long enough for Dad to get a little bit worried, just long enough to maybe get him to feel bad about what he'd said. I reached the top of the fort, and a voice in the darkness said, "Funny meeting you here, my good man!"

CHAPTER 31

I SCREAMED. BEFORE I COULD STOP MYSELF, BEFORE MY brain processed that "Funny meeting you here, my good man" was probably not axe-murderer-speak, before I realized that for whatever reason Finn was in the fort at nine o'clock at night, and so was I.

Finn grabbed my arm, which was a good thing, because there was so much adrenaline pumping through my body that I was about to lift off into outer space. I stopped screaming and panted as I slowly began to return to earth. "What are you doing here? Where have you been?"

"Court," Finn said simply.

It wasn't the answer I'd expected; it was also an unusually simple response for Finn. I'd thought for sure he would say something about joining up with a traveling circus or being abducted by an international spy ring. "Oh," I said, my heart still pounding in my chest, "how come?"

"Custody dispute, following the death of my paternal grandparents last year." I nodded. I knew a little bit about custody stuff from kids whose parents got divorced. "But it's all resolved now that they know I didn't inherit anything of worth," Finn continued. "Neither of them wants me, so I am, as you might say, a free man. Of course, not legally. I can apply for full emancipation at age sixteen."

"Oh." I didn't know what to say. "Is that good? I mean, are you okay with that?"

"It's as I expected," Finn said.

The matter-of-fact way he said it made it sadder than if his voice had been froggy with tears.

"Why are you here? I mean now?"

"I live nearby. It's a group home and very loud—especially at night. Sometimes I come here just to think."

"It's really cold out," I said, observing the puffs of air leaving my mouth with each breath.

"It's *very* loud there," Finn said. "Why are you here, Lucas?"

"I got in a fight with my dad. I didn't know where else to go."

"Well, it's fortuitous that you found me here. As it happens, I have something for you. If you don't mind a bit of noise, that is."

I followed Finn down the ladder and through the woods on an icy trail that glistened in the moonlight. I didn't know the street where we came out, but Finn whistled to himself as we made one turn and then another through the neighborhood. Finally we arrived in front of a square two-story house with one red and one green porch light. The car parked in the driveway was at a funny angle and poking a little bit into a snowbank, as though the driver had been too late coming home to park carefully.

Finn pushed the door open, and we passed through an entryway lined with hooks hanging heavy with jackets, and countless pairs of boots and shoes. Finn's walk was different as he led me into the kitchen—his shoulders rounded over, his step less jaunty than usual. In the kitchen there were two round tables pressed together and a young woman poring over a thick textbook. Her face lit up when she looked up and saw us. "How was your walk, buddy?" she asked Finn. I had never heard anyone talk to Finn like that.

"Fine, thanks," Finn responded. "Natalie, this is Lucas. He's a friend from school."

Natalie beamed as she looked at both of us. She wrote

something down on a clipboard stuffed with curling pages. "Okay, kids," she said. "It's a little late for a school night. Lucas, do your parents know you're here?"

"Um, I'm going to call," I said, sidestepping the question.

"Okay," she said. "Well, it's really nice to meet you. We all love Finn so much."

Finn Clark did something I'd never seen him do before. He blushed all across his cheeks and the tips of his ears, which lit up like a stop sign. I followed Finn out of the kitchen as Natalie called after us, "Steer clear of Taylor's room; she's having a hard night."

I followed Finn through a dining room that had been converted into a kind of study. There were two desks facing each other, each with an older desktop computer and one with a printer covered by a piece of paper with the words *not working* scrawled across it in purple crayon. We went up the stairs. There was a shiny, dark-colored wood banister and a faded rug at the top that suggested maybe, once upon a time, the house had been well cared for. There was paint chipping on all the doors we passed. Really loud, angry music was pumping out of one of them. *Stay out!* was written on a small dry-erase board stuck to the door. I figured this was probably Taylor's room and the source of a lot of the noise Finn had mentioned.

At the end of the hall Finn let me into a small, narrow room with a loft bed covered with a plaid comforter. A few button-down shirts hung on one of those portable metal racks. On the windowsill were some toiletry items, lined up neatly in a row. I picked up a brown wooden brush without a handle.

"Shoe-polishing kit," Finn said, and I nodded, because even if it wasn't normal, it was normal for Finn. He gestured to two chairs that were set up underneath the loft bed. I sank down into one of them. Some springs squawked, but it was comfortable enough. There was a bookshelf under the bed, and I recognized some of the titles as books I'd seen Finn reading in the tree fort. Finn sat across from me and crossed one leg on top of the other; he held his hands so his fingertips pressed together. We both looked around at the small space he had carved out and made his own.

"How long have you, um, lived here?"

"Just since September, and so far it's not so bad. I have my own quarters, as you can see." He reached behind him and pulled out a notebook, from which he tore a single page. *Riverview Psychiatric Facility* was written on it, along with a phone number. "I believe this is where your mom is staying," he said.

I stared silently at the words for several minutes before

I could summon any of my own. "How?" I managed to croak out.

"Well, you said your aunt lived in western Massachusetts, so I started calling around and asking for a patient named Alexandra Barnes."

"And they just told you that?"

Finn coughed. "Not exactly." He lowered his voice and said, "They told Dr. Phineas Clark from Inter-Med General Practitioners, who was following up on a patient referral."

My hand holding the paper shook. If Finn noticed, he didn't say anything about it. "You should probably call your dad," he said gently. "So he knows where you are."

Where I am, and where I'm going, I thought as I stared at the paper in my hand.

CHAPTER 32

I CALLED DAD AND HE CAME AND PICKED ME UP WITHOUT saying anything after asking for the address.

"Are you okay?" he asked, when I got in the truck.

"Yeah," I said, which was far from the truth but all that I felt like telling him. I put my seat belt on and wedged my shoulders into the space between the seat and the window. I focused on the white line running down the side of the road in the darkness. When we turned into Oak Hill, something cracked in me and I felt big tears slide down my cheeks.

"Why is Mom in a psychiatric hospital? What's wrong with her? If she was so sick, why did you let her leave?"

"Oh, geez, Lucas," Dad said. "I didn't know what else to do."

"Well, I know where Mom is, and I want to go see her."

Dad didn't say anything, but his hands tightened on the steering wheel.

The next morning, I jerked awake with no idea where I was or what day it was. I looked at my clock. It was eight. I had more than missed the bus; it was already halfway through first period. I rushed out of my room and there was Dad sitting on the couch, his feet propped up on the coffee table, one big toe poking through a hole in his white sweat sock. He hadn't shaved in a few days, and the hair on his face was a mix of gray and brown. The lines in the corner of his eyes looked especially creased. It was like he'd woken up older, or maybe I just hadn't really looked at him in a long time.

"Don't you have work?" I asked.

"I'm going in late. I called your aunt Sheila." He said it like he was describing cleaning the toilet. "And I got you a bus ticket. You have to switch buses in Boston, and Sheila will pick you up in Northampton. You think you can handle that?"

I nodded vigorously.

"Don't talk to anybody weird. If you need help, you ask the bus driver. They'll know you're by yourself. I'll drive you to Portsmouth, so we need to leave in about an hour."

I took a step back, but then Dad leaned forward on the couch. "Lucas, I lied," he said. "About Mom not wanting you. She wanted you to come with her. She was going to have you live with Sheila, and I don't know what her plan was, but she had a plan. I wouldn't let her. I saw the shape she was in, and I didn't think it would be good for you. I'm sorry."

He rubbed his forehead with his hand. "I always had Charlie, and you had your mom. I figured it was a phase, and you and I would, you know . . . in time. I—I didn't want to lose another . . ." But his voice trailed off.

I knew what he was saying, but I couldn't find pity in the stew of emotions that was swirling in my chest. I was furious.

"I just . . . I knew you would choose her. You've always picked her, ever since you were little—and I don't blame you," he rushed to add. "I'd probably pick her too if I had the choice between the two of us as parents. You and me, we're kinda similar. Quiet. I never know what to say, really. With Charlie it wasn't a big deal. He was always talking, so I could just, you know, be there."

I couldn't help it—I rolled my eyes. I didn't want or need this to be about Charlie.

Dad went on. "I thought, you know, if you and I had some time . . ." He gestured in front of him like we were both supposed to envision some great relationship that would develop between us. "But I just don't think—I don't have anything." This conversation was getting weirder and weirder. Dad was jealous of me and Mom? Dad thought he was like *me*? Was that supposed to make me feel worse or better?

My fingers were itching to start packing. I'd have plenty of time to think about it all on the bus.

"I'll be back on Sunday," I said. He looked immediately relieved, and I wondered if he had thought that maybe I wouldn't ever come back. "I've got school."

"Sure, right. I'll pick you up."

I threw some clothes and my toothbrush into a backpack with my Ranger's Apprentice library book, more evidence that I would, in fact, be returning. "Call the school," I yelled out to Dad, "so they know I'm excused." A thought occurred to me, and I stuck my head out in the hall. "And can we stop by Robbie's house on the way?"

Dad grumbled about possible traffic in Portsmouth, but he stopped at Robbie's house like I asked him to.

"Make it quick," he warned.

As soon as I got to the door and rang the bell, I realized my mistake. It was Friday morning and Robbie would be at school already. But before I could turn and go, his mom was at the door, her computer in hand. The same boy from the picture in the kitchen was smiling pleasantly out of the screen.

"Lucas," Robbie's mom said, "Robbie's not here right now, honey. He's at school. Shouldn't you be there too?"

"Um," I said, but before I could explain, she interrupted.

"This is Pascal, my fifth baby!" She pointed the screen at me. "He's such a sweetheart. We FaceTime every week! He never forgets." Pascal waved at me and I waved back. "He just got his exams back and he did so well," Mrs. Belcher went on. "This is Robbie's friend Lucas. Will you show him your report card, sweetie?" Pascal looked a little embarrassed, but he held up a paper with row after row of grades in the high nineties.

"Wow," I said appreciatively.

"Robbie will be home after school. Do you want me to give him a message? Or, here"—she thrust a pad of paper and a pen in my hand—"you can leave him a note. I promise not to read it."

"Okay," I said.

Robbie's mom took her computer back inside and left me on the porch to write my note.

Hey, it worked! I'm going to see my mom. Tell everyone I'll be back on Monday.

After I handed over the note and waved goodbye to Pascal, it occurred to me that Robbie wouldn't get the note until the end of the school day, so he wouldn't see everyone until Monday anyway.

"When you call the school, can you ask Mrs. Kelley to tell my friends I'm okay?"

Dad gave me a funny look. I shrugged. "Sometimes they get worried."

CHAPTER 33

AUNT SHEILA WAS THERE TO PICK ME UP. "HOW WAS YOUR ride?" she asked me after a quick side hug.

"It was okay," I told her, which was mostly the truth. An older lady with purple streaks in her hair sat next to me from Boston to Northampton and told me a lot of stories about her cats and the abandoned or abused horses she took care of. She referred to all of them by name and seemed to expect that I knew who she was talking about when she said things like "Marlon loves carrots and apples" or "Brutus doesn't like to have his shoes cleaned out." When I finally took out my DS and started playing *Mario Kart*, she wrinkled her nose but then left me alone.

Aunt Sheila unlocked her shiny red Lincoln Continental

and gave me a funny look when I reached for the handle on the passenger door. "Are you old enough to sit up front?

"I'm almost twelve," I told her, but she still looked at me as if I might be trying to get away with something. We hadn't been to visit Aunt Sheila since before Charlie died. Dad never liked to go. Sheila and her husband always lectured Mom about financial responsibility. After Charlie died, I knew that Mom and Aunt Sheila had some kind of fight, although I didn't know what it was actually about.

Sheila and Uncle Robert ran a dental practice. Sheila was the dentist and Uncle Robert did the books for her. They didn't have any kids and went on a lot of cruises. Before Charlie died, they used to send me fifty dollars for Christmas and on my birthday. But Sheila was never warm, and I noticed that she still smelled faintly like toothpaste and the powder that came inside rubber gloves. When she drove, she leaned over the steering wheel of her car like a much shorter person might do, or maybe someone who was just overly concerned about hitting squirrels.

"I don't know how much your father has told you," she said as we proceeded at a glacially slow pace out of the parking lot. "Your mother is making very good progress at Riverview. And I'm just grateful that Robert and I have the means to help her." She paused, and I had a sense that this was the moment when I was supposed to express my gratitude, but I stared out at the road and said nothing. What was I supposed to say? *Thank you for taking my mother away from me?*

"Why hasn't she called?"

Aunt Sheila pursed her lips. "Your mother has been in a very dark place, Lucas. We can't blame her for it. She's been through so much since your brother died. She hasn't been healthy. Your uncle Robert and I didn't think it was a good idea for her to be in contact with you until she was more stable."

My face got hot. What did they know about kids and what might be good for me, anyway? "What about her *doctor?*"

"We're all on the same page about this." She paused and gave a tight smile. "What's important is that she's better, she's getting better. She's living with us now and going to Riverview every day for what's called outpatient services."

"Services for what?" I interrupted. "What's actually wrong with her?"

Sheila took a deep breath and glanced at me as if trying to determine whether sitting up front made me old enough to know the truth. "Alex—your mom—she's had this in her forever. Since we were teenagers. Her senior year of high school was the worst. She barely graduated. I was one year behind her. I saw it all. She just wanted to go off and party with your dad and pretend like the dark times never happened. But then there were weeks—a month, once—where she could barely get out of bed. She would try and get dressed and just that would make her overwhelmed. She cried all the time."

"About what?"

"It's chemical, honey. Something in her chemistry isn't balanced right. That's part of what the doctors are trying to figure out. I'll let her share more about that with you. I need to go back to the office, so you'll have the whole afternoon together."

Aunt Sheila lived in a development marked by a stone entrance and a green sign that said Private Way. The houses all resembled each other, but some had the garage on the left instead of the right, and a few had two chimneys or a slightly different set of big windows facing the street. We pulled up into Aunt Sheila's steep driveway and Mom came rushing out. She was biting her fingers—she had almost her whole hand in her mouth—and I could see she was already crying. I didn't even wait for the car to stop all the way, and I vaguely heard Sheila squawking at me as I bolted for Mom.

I wrapped my arms around her and buried my face in her shoulder. I felt her chest shaking, or maybe it was me shaking her. Sheila hovered around us, threatening to drag us inside if we didn't come in or get our coats and hats. But I couldn't let go. I was crying. I could feel the tears dampening Mom's shoulder. I tried to breathe her in—she still smelled the same, the flowers of her shampoo and her skin like a soft, warm pillowcase from the dryer. Finally, we pulled away a little bit and let ourselves be led inside. Mom didn't let go of me as we walked in, arms wrapped around each other's sides. Had I grown? Mom seemed smaller—skinnier, for sure. She was wearing an ugly blue sweater that I guessed was probably Sheila's. It had snow-flakes on it and a sledding bear.

Sheila hovered around us in the kitchen. She made us sandwiches, and even though it was between lunch and dinner, I wolfed mine down. Mom just picked little pieces of chicken salad out from between the two pieces of bread. Sheila made a comment about Mom not eating enough, and Mom shot her a look, which got her quiet for a little while.

"I need to go back into work," she said in a too loud voice. "But you and Lucas can go walk around the arbo-retum. Remember we thought that might be nice? And then we can meet back here for dinner around six." Was

Mom going to say anything about the weird way Sheila was talking to her? When Sheila finally left the room to go to work, Mom sagged like a deflated balloon.

"Sorry, Lucas, I'm really tired."

There were dark circles around her eyes I hadn't noticed at first. "It's okay," I said. "Do you want to go for a walk like Aunt Sheila said?"

Mom brightened up again when we left the house bundled up in our coats and hats. A light snow was falling, and everything looked like it was dusted with powdered sugar. Mom stuck her arm through mine and pulled me close.

"It's so good to hold you, sweetie," she said. She leaned over and stuck her nose in my hair just behind my ear. "Your babies have a smell. As long as I live, I'll always love your smell." I was wondering if Charlie and I smelled the same, but I wasn't going to ask. I didn't want to risk upsetting her.

We turned into the arboretum, a big park near Aunt Sheila's house that was famous for having tree specimens from around the world. The branches of most of the trees were white or gray against a white sky. Mom took a deep breath like she was trying to suck in all the air of the world. "What can I tell you, Lucas?" Her voice was small but steady.

"Um," I hesitated, "I mean, I know you were sad, because of Charlie. And then you got really sad. And then you left.

But you seem better now. You seem a lot better, so I don't really get it. I don't understand why you had to go and why you couldn't call, and why you can't come back?" This was what I had planned on saying—exactly the way I'd mapped it out in my head on the bus. But now it didn't sound right. After what Sheila had told me, maybe this was about more than just Charlie.

"I seem better?" Mom asked. "That's good. That's really good. I feel better. Some of the time." She seemed to be considering each word carefully. "And I really miss you, sweetie. I miss you so much. I wanted you to come with me, but Dad talked me out of it. And he was right."

I rolled my eyes and shook my head.

"He *was* right. It would have been incredibly selfish to drag you here. You would have had to live with Sheila and Rob and start at a new school, and I didn't know—I didn't know how I would be." She twisted her hands together.

"You seem fine," I said stubbornly. But I had noticed how red her fingers were and the way her fingernails had been bitten down to nearly nothing.

We walked together arm in arm for a while. I thought about a lot of things I could say, but I wasn't sure. She did seem better, but her good mood felt like a thin shell, and I didn't know what was underneath. Finally, I asked something that had been bothering me. "Was Charlie smart?"

Mom pulled me closer, snuggling my arm. "Yes."

"Was he a good student?"

Mom laughed, and I was glad that talking about Charlie didn't seem to be making anything worse. "Well, some of the time. He definitely got some doozies on some tests. But his teachers always let him make things up. You know, everyone loved Charlie."

"Well, Ms. Edgerly said—"

But before I could continue Mom interrupted. "Oh boy, you've been talking to Rachel Edgerly, huh? She loved your brother, but she could be a real pain in the butt. She was always calling us about this or the other thing. It kind of got on my nerves after a while. I mean, like she thought he was *her* kid or something."

"Well, she said she thought he might have had ADHD. And that's why he had a hard time in school."

"That's it. That's what she was always going on about. Trying to diagnose him with something fancy. He was a kid. Sometimes he didn't study. Sometimes he just wanted to play outside, you know? But she didn't accept that. Wanted us to sign a whole bunch of papers to have him tested. There wasn't anything wrong with him."

I wasn't going to argue. I couldn't take Ms. Edgerly's side against Mom. But I did wonder.

"Charlie and I were a lot alike. Sometimes we just have our heads in the clouds. Teachers used to always say that to me." And then her face got sad and she said, "Had. Charlie *had* his head in the clouds."

"It's okay, Mom," I said. "We don't have to talk about it anymore."

But it was like she didn't hear me, and her grip on my arm got looser. "You're more like your father, Lucas. You're steady like he is."

There it was again. It made the acid in my stomach churn. Me and Mom were supposed to be alike, and Charlie was like Dad, athletic and popular or whatever else Dad was. I wasn't going to let her get away with changing everything about the past just because she was depressed or whatever. But before I could speak, she said, "You know, you're right. Maybe we shouldn't talk about it anymore."

We walked back without talking. It was peaceful mostly. Except for a thought that was nagging me, popping up like an icon for an app that you can't seem to quit. What if it wasn't the similarities between two people that made them close? What if Dad and I butted heads because we were similar, like he said, and Mom and I were close because we were different, and needed something that the other person had? I didn't like to think about it. How was a person ever supposed to get to be whole?

CHAPTER 34

DINNER WITH UNCLE ROBERT AND AUNT SHEILA WAS OKAY.
They talked a lot about their cruise last summer in Alaska. Uncle Robert kept passing me his phone to show me pictures that were supposed to be orcas but looked more like water with some dark shapes in it. But I nodded and said it was cool, and that seemed to make him happy. I kept glancing over at Mom, who seemed to be getting smaller and smaller in her chair. She wasn't eating; she just kept lifting her fork and then putting it down or moving her food from one side of the plate to the other. Every so often Sheila would nag her to eat and she would smile, like she'd forgotten something, and actually put a small bite of food in her mouth.

Aunt Sheila asked me about school; she and Uncle Robert acted really interested when I talked about it. It seemed like they got most of their ideas about kids and school from Fox News, because they kept asking me about things like "cyberbullying" and "hazing" and they would actually hold up their hands and do the air quotes. They had to tell me what hazing was because I had never heard that word. I told them that there were mean kids, sure, but a lot of kids were nice, too—which they accepted even though they looked at me like I was hiding something.

I told them a little bit about Finn, Robbie, Cat, and Anna. They particularly liked hearing about Finn. When I told them about how he dressed up as Andy Warhol for Halloween, Uncle Robert hooted and said, "What a character!" Mom brightened and sat up taller when I talked about school too, so I kept talking. After a little while, though, she said she had a headache and needed to lie down.

"But you'll miss dessert!" Aunt Sheila protested.

Mom just smiled weakly and left the table. Dessert was really good. I ate two helpings of the brownie sundaes Aunt Sheila made with homemade whipped cream. After dinner Uncle Robert asked if I wanted to watch a movie with him. It was an old movie called *Die Hard* that Uncle Robert said every kid should watch because it was a classic.

I really just wanted to go talk to Mom, but every time I went to the bathroom and walked past her door, it was closed. At one point I found Aunt Sheila standing there, wringing her hands and talking to Mom through the door.

"This is what I was worried about," she said. But I wasn't sure what exactly *this* was, so I didn't say anything.

After the movie, I walked slowly by Mom's door one more time. I stopped and knocked lightly. "Mom?"

"Yes, sweetie" came the muffled reply.

"Will you come tuck me in?"

There was a long pause, then the sound of a nose blowing and shuffling feet. "I'll be there in just a minute."

I brushed my teeth and pulled back the covers on Aunt Sheila's blue-and-white-patterned guest bed. The pillows were soft, and immediately my eyelids felt heavy.

Mom came padding in and lay down next to me so we were face-to-face. Her hazel eyes were wide and clear, and her bangs had a few flecks of gray in them I hadn't noticed before. She reached over and ran one finger down the bridge of my nose, landing with a finger kiss on my lips. "Hi, buddy," she said. I smiled. "You're going to sleep well tonight."

"Are you?"

Mom looked pained, but she didn't turn away. "I don't

know. My brain is swirling. It's a lot."

I nodded. "I know. I feel like that sometimes too."

"And sometimes," Mom said, "I start worrying I won't be able to fall asleep. And then I'll be tired and feel bad, and . . ."

"I know. I get it," I said.

"I wish you didn't," Mom said. "I feel like I gave it to you, all that thinking and worrying."

"It's not your fault," I said. And I looked right at her and she looked right back at me. "I'm not just parts of Dad and parts of you. I'm my own thing." As I said it, I knew that I wanted to believe it was true. I was saying it for her, but I was also saying it for myself.

"You're amazing, kiddo," she said. And she brushed the hair off my forehead with her fingertips. A single tear collected in the corner of her eye. It just pooled and nestled there like a jewel. I closed my eyes, and Mom continued to brush her hand through my hair until I fell asleep.

CHAPTER 35

I WOKE UP TO AUNT SHEILA GENTLY SHAKING MY SHOUL-
der. "Good morning, Lucas," she said. There was a small
glass of orange juice on the table next to me. "I didn't know
if you liked orange juice." I nodded, sat up, and took a small
sip. Aunt Sheila was dressed already, her shoulder-length
brown hair hanging together in one simple shape.

"Are you going to work?" I asked.

"Yes, eventually," she said. "I use Saturdays to catch up
on paperwork and ordering. Lucas, your mom's in a hard
place this morning."

"What do you mean?"

"She's very down." She paused. "You must understand
this isn't your fault." She looked up at the ceiling and out

the window. Anywhere but directly at me. "I was afraid this would happen. She's just so fragile right now, and she takes everything so personally, and then there's just no talking to her. I woke you up because I'm going to bring her to Riverview this morning. I already called and arranged things for her. It's just that it might be hard to see. I wanted to warn you that she might not seem like herself. You don't have to come with us. Uncle Robert will be here, and there might be some cartoons on or something."

"No, it's okay. I want to come with you. But when is Mom coming back?"

"This evening," Aunt Sheila said. "Most likely. Robert might be able to take some time this afternoon and bring you over to the college or the art museum." My bus was supposed to leave Sunday morning. That wouldn't give us very much time. "Let's just see how things go, okay, Lucas?"

I nodded because I didn't really have a choice. I took my toothbrush and walked down the hall to the bathroom. The door to Mom's room was open a crack, and I could hear little bits of muffled conversation.

"It's okay, Alex," Aunt Sheila was saying. "You need to get dressed so we can go. No, you don't have to come down for breakfast. I told him. No, he wasn't upset. He's okay, Alex. Try not to start this again." I could hear the sounds of Mom crying. I walked quicker and left the faucet running while I brushed my teeth. I got dressed and ate my breakfast while Uncle Robert read the paper and made weird grunting noises about whatever he was reading.

When I was done, I cleared my place and cleaned up the crumbs around my plate with the paper napkin. "Wow," Uncle Robert said, "you're some kind of teenager, kid. Forget what they say on the news about your generation. I'm very impressed." I smiled because it was nice and also because Uncle Robert was nice but pretty clueless. I heard Aunt Sheila in the hall ushering Mom out to the car. I grabbed a piece of toast in case she wanted it and then ran back upstairs to get my coat.

I slid into the seat behind Mom and handed up the piece of toast I'd saved her. "Thank you, sweetie," she said in a tight, sad voice I didn't recognize. "I'm so sorry, Lucas," she started to say, but it was lost in a sob. I reached forward and put my hand on her shoulder, and she gripped my hand in hers. It was warm but clammy with tears. We drove like that all the way to Riverview, with me leaning forward awkwardly because I didn't want to let go of Mom and I didn't want her to let go of me.

Riverview looked like a weird cross between a hotel and a doctor's office. Aunt Sheila pulled into a space marked

Patient Drop-Off and unclicked her seat belt. She turned to look at us and said, "I think you two should say your goodbyes here."

Mom released my hand and we got out of the car. I was almost as tall as her now, but I lowered my head to her chest so she could hug me. "I'll probably just take the bus back today," I said. I waited, hoping she would argue with me, hoping she would tell me to wait until she got back. But she didn't. She just nodded into the top of my head and kissed me and stroked my hair.

"I'll be better the next time," she whispered into my cheek. "I promise, I'll be better the next time."

I watched as Aunt Sheila walked her to the door. Mom let herself be shuffled along. I watched until I couldn't see them any longer. Part of me wanted to run after her, to grab her and stuff her in my backpack and drag her back to Maine with me. But part of me could see that Aunt Sheila was right. Mom needed to be here. At least for now.

CHAPTER 36

I DIDN'T WANT TO GO TO THE ART MUSEUM OR EVEN watch movies with Uncle Robert. I wasn't sure how I would feel if Mom came home worse than when I left her—I didn't want this sad shadow of Mom eclipsing all my good memories of her—so I asked Aunt Sheila if I could take the bus home that afternoon instead. She didn't argue with me about it, so we went back to the house and I packed up the few things I had brought with me.

Aunt Sheila bought me a couple of candy bars and some comics from the mini mall next to the bus station. Before she could say anything, I hugged her and told her I was glad I came. I didn't want her to feel bad about me having a lousy time. I hadn't. I mean, I'd had a weird time, but that wasn't the same thing.

"Tell Uncle Robert goodbye for me," I said. "Maybe next time we can watch *Die Hard Two*."

Aunt Sheila smiled. "That would make both of us very happy. I called your father—well, I texted him. He knows when to meet your bus." There was nothing else for me to do, so I got on the bus and waved and watched as Sheila drove very slowly out of the parking lot. There were no weird cat ladies to sit next to—in fact, I had two whole seats to myself. I watched some confusing movies from the nineties or whenever it was that they big hair and ugly sweaters. I didn't even follow the plot; I just sort of listened and watched the people on the screen move through their lives.

I could feel my brain shifting around the pieces of what had happened in the last twenty-four hours like some kind of odd chess game, trying to make sense of it all. It was exhausting. I pressed my face against the cool glass of the bus window and watched the highway glide by.

When Dad picked me up at the bus, he pulled me into a big hug and kissed the top of my head. Up until that point I'd been holding it together pretty well, but that hug from

Dad kind of put me over the edge and I started crying, like really blubbering and making a big snotty mess of myself. I expected Dad to get all uncomfortable and weird, but he didn't. He hugged me and didn't let go. Maybe he didn't have the words, but he didn't let go. I thought about what Mom had said about him being steady.

He didn't turn any music on in the truck. And even though we didn't say much, there weren't any fake words either. Instead of going home, Dad took us right from the bus to Walmart and bought me three new pairs of jeans and a new winter jacket. "You got bigger" was all he said, but there was something about the way he said it, like he wasn't talking about just the way my clothes fit.

The next day was Sunday, so I sat around in my pajamas thinking about everything I was going to tell Finn, Robbie, Cat, and Anna. When Dad got back from his errands, he handed me a phone. It was nothing fancy, just one step above a flip phone, like the kind we'd used to text Anna's mom. "It's for you and Mom," he said. "I already put her number in, and mine."

I opened the phone. There was a message already waiting for me from Mom.

Hi Sweetie

Hi Mom how r u

Better. I'm sorry you had to leave early

It's ok

I love you

Me too

I looked up at Dad. "Doesn't this cost a lot of money?"

"It's not that bad," he said.

I took the phone to my room and set it carefully on the shelf next to an acorn cap I'd found last week or the week before, and I smiled.

CHAPTER 37

ANNA CAME RUNNING UP TO ME FIRST THING ON MONDAY
morning and grabbed me by the shoulders. "Did you go?"
she squealed. "Finn's back! And he told us that he gave
you the information about your mom, and then Robbie
messaged me about your note, but I've just been dying to
know what happened. So, did you go?"

"Yes."

"Oh my God! I knew it!" I smiled, as much at Anna's
excitement as anything else. "So how was it? How was she?
I mean, you don't have to tell me if you don't want to, but
that would be really annoying. Okay, you do have to tell me
just a little bit."

"It was good. I mean, it was okay. It was good to see

her, but she's not that good. She's in a hospital, and she's sad a lot. I guess she really needs to be there."

Anna's face got soft. "I'm sure she's sad because she's away from you. I mean, you're her kid, and you're like a really good person." Anna smiled nervously, and then I blushed because of what Anna was saying. Thankfully, Mrs. Lynch called everyone to their seats before anything could get more awkward than it already was. Anna sat at Robbie's table and I watched her face light up as she whispered to him intently throughout Mrs. Lynch's opening directions on how to write a conclusion to our theme essays.

"Denouement," Mrs. Lynch announced. She was saying it in a funny voice. "That's French—does anyone know what it means?" She was pointing to the last part of the plot diagram.

"The end?" Sadie Gillespie ventured a guess.

"Good idea," Mrs. Lynch said, "but it's more than that. The literal translation from French means 'the unknotting of things.' So the author tells us a story and presents us with a big knot—that's our conflict. And then by the end of the book we have the denouement: the unknotting of things. Can anyone think of an example of this from the book we've been reading?"

Some hands went up, but I was thinking about my

stomach, about the knot *I'd* been feeling since Mom left: a combination of loneliness, confusion, and fear. Was it gone? I rubbed my chest and belly. I patted my pocket where my phone was tucked away, set to silent mode for school. I *did* feel better, but there was something else, a snag in the line still kinked and folded over, something we hadn't fixed yet and I wasn't sure that we could.

Finn actually came to lunch, but he was quiet. He brightened up when I told him about my visit with Mom and the phone that Dad got me. He seemed genuinely pleased and said, "Well done, old chap." But when Cat started talking about her travel basketball team, he seemed to fade out again.

I nudged him under the table with my foot and asked, "Something wrong?"

For a second, I thought he might put on the Finn mask and brush me off, but instead he sighed and said, "Natalie's leaving."

I thought for a second. "Natalie who works at, um, your house?"

He nodded. "And it's not just that. They're making cuts. Natalie said there aren't enough kids in this area to justify keeping the house open. They're looking to combine it with another home in Biddeford. That place is newer and nicer, but . . ."

"You'd have to move again. It's not that far away," I added, but it wasn't much consolation to a kid without a car, or parents to drive him.

"No, it's not," Finn said. "I've never really minded moving before. But I've never really had friends before." He twiddled half-heartedly with his plastic straw before submerging it in his milk carton. "I suppose Steinbeck was right when he said you can never really go home. It 'has ceased to exist, except in the mothballs of memory.'"

I didn't know what to do. He was soaked in sadness like a cookie sopped in milk and about to crumble. When Finn left to return his tray, I turned to everyone else at the table. "We've got to do something for Finn!" I laid out his situation as quickly as I could.

Finn was heading back toward our table. Anna leaned forward and whispered, "Everyone get to the library during last period. Get the bathroom pass if you have to, but meet me there about fifteen minutes after the bell," she said.

CHAPTER 38

"I DON'T HAVE THAT MUCH TIME," ROBBIE SAID. HE WAS holding the fuzzy green parrot that was the health teacher's bathroom pass.

"What are our options?" Cat said.

"I did a little searching at the beginning of class when we were supposed to be doing an online review game," Anna said. "Finn needs a guardian. He needs someone to take him in, and then he could stay."

"Like adopt him?" I said skeptically.

"Not necessarily," Anna said. "Maybe just be a foster family. And then, if they like him, they could adopt him."

"Finn would be a really easy kid to have around," Cat said. "I mean, I bet his room is super neat."

"But what does it take to like qualify as a foster family?" I said.

"We're going to need help," Anna said. "I'll make an appointment with guidance. Same time tomorrow. Maybe Mrs. Verzoni can help us with the details."

Mrs. Verzoni eyed us suspiciously when we all turned up in her office. She was a small, sharp woman with black hair and flashing eyes. "Is there a test? Usually when kids show up in big groups it's because they're trying to get out of a test."

"No test," I said.

"We're not even in the same class right now," Robbie said.

"We actually need your help," Cat said.

Mrs. Verzoni looked at us a second time and then smiled welcomingly. "Okay, kids, what's up?"

We sat down around her round conference table. "We want to help Finn Clark get a family," I said.

"Oh, wow! Okay, kids. Well, listen, that's very sweet, but I really can't discuss another student's family situation with you."

"We already know," I said. "We know he's living in a group home. We know he doesn't have a family, and we know he's probably going to have to move again."

"It's not fair," Anna said. "Finn's helped us all solve a lot of problems, and now he's got a big problem, and we just need some help figuring out how we can help him."

"Can't you just talk about it with us, like, hyperactively? You know, without using his name?" Robbie asked.

Mrs. Verzoni brought her hand up to her mouth to hide a smile. "You mean hypothetically, honey?"

"Exactly!" Robbie said. "That's what I said."

Mrs. Verzoni sighed. "Finding a foster family for a child is not a simple process. Potential parents have to submit an application, go through a mandatory eighteen-to-twenty-four-hour training, complete a home visit. They have to get fingerprinted and background-checked. There's a lot to it."

Robbie smiled, undeterred. "But hypothetically"—he pronounced it carefully this time—"we could find someone."

I could tell Mrs. Verzoni didn't think this was such a great idea. "I guess so. But I wouldn't get your hopes up."

"Let's make a list," Anna said. "Write down every adult you know who might be a good match." She paused. "Or just every adult you know."

We wrote down all the teachers we liked and even a few who seemed just okay. Robbie put his parents down as a possibility. "I mean, my dad said he didn't want any more babies, but this is different."

I racked my brain for someone to write down. I knew Dad would never go for it in a million years. "Can they be old?" I asked Mrs. Verzoni.

"Sure. Pretty much any adult can do it—single, married, seniors, people in a same-sex relationship—as long as you can pass all the other stuff."

"Write down the Boudreaus," I said. It was a long shot, but I was pretty sure they could afford it, and I knew they had the room.

At the end of the period Mrs. Verzoni ushered us out of her office with our list, and a warning. "Careful not to get his hopes up too much, kids. In fact, I'd advise you not to mention what you're doing unless you have a very serious prospect."

"And it will ruin the surprise," Anna said. I wished I had her confidence. I thought about what I would say to the Boudreaus. How did you even start this conversation? I was supposed to be going to gym, but I was already super late. Instead I found myself wandering toward Ms. Edgerly's room. I peeked in, and at first I thought it was empty, but then I caught sight of her in the back tinkering with part of the living machine.

"Hey," she called, "can you pass me the fish food?"

I found the yellow container on the table and passed

it behind the fish tank. Ms. Edgerly shook some into the tank and I watched as the fish swam to the surface, moving their mouths in little sucking motions to gobble up the papery flakes.

"Where are you supposed to be? Last time I checked, wandering around the halls wasn't a class."

"It's a recent addition."

She smirked. "Seriously, Lucas, where are you supposed to be?"

"Gym."

"Oh, okay. What's up?"

"Could you adopt Finn?" I didn't even realize I was going to say it before I blurted it out. "I mean, be his foster parent. Could you do that? Would you do that?"

"Ha!" Ms. Edgerly barked. "Oh wait, you're serious, aren't you? Lucas, I don't have kids. I don't. I mean, that's not something I . . ." Ms. Edgerly was flustered and flapping her hands around as she tried to explain. "Wait a minute. What's going on? Is Finn okay? Have you talked to Mrs. Verzoni about this?"

"Yes, we did. We're trying to solve a problem for Finn. The house where he lives is going to close and he's going to have to move again, and we're the only friends he's ever had, and he's one of the only friends I've ever had, so I know how I'd feel if I was about to lose everybody." I was babbling. This was nuts. I shook my head. "Never mind. I'm sorry I bothered you with this. It's too impossible. We fixed some things, but this is too big." I started to walk toward the door.

"What do you mean, you fixed some things?" Ms. Edgerly called after me.

I turned around and dug an acorn cap out of my pocket. "I'll tell you, but can you write me a note for missing class?"

CHAPTER 39

NO ONE EVER SAID WE COULDN'T TELL ABOUT THE ACORN caps—we just never did. I sat down across the desk from Ms. Edgerly and told her the whole thing. She shook her head appreciatively when I told her about Cat's hair. When I told her about the burping thing with Greg Hutchins, she whispered, "Brilliant," and covered her mouth to stifle a laugh. Her eyes widened when I told her about Anna's mom and the secret cell phone, and then I got to my part of the story.

"So I wanted my mom back," I started, even though I knew that wasn't the beginning of the story. But this was Ms. Edgerly, and she'd been part of our story for a long time,

so I started over. "Since Charlie died, my mom's been . . ."
I had to stop because I realized I was telling this for the
first time. I wasn't sure what words I really wanted to use.
"My mom had to go away, to get better. But she didn't tell
me. She just left me and my dad, and I guess"—my aunt
Sheila's words came out of my mouth—"she was in really
bad shape. Maybe it wasn't just Charlie. Maybe this was a
part of her I never really knew."

Ms. Edgerly stared at me intently, and I felt weird.
The way she was looking at me was like she was seeing
something that she hadn't seen before. "Lucas, I'm so sorry.
That sounds really hard. I can't believe . . ." Her voice trailed
off. "I had no idea."

"Do you want to have kids ever?"

"Oh," she said, sounding surprised. "I think so, one
day. My wife and I, we've talked about it."

I thought for a second I'd misheard her. I looked over
at her desk and suddenly saw all the photos of her with the
slender brown-skinned woman with short dark hair in a
different way. That wasn't just her best friend with her in
the double kayak or locked arm in arm watching a sunset
on a beach somewhere.

"But, Lucas, I'm a teacher and I try really hard to be

a good teacher. And part of that is knowing that I can't save people." She paused. "I've made that mistake before."

"I know that. I really do. But Finn doesn't need you to save him. He needs someone to care about him, and that's not the same thing as saving someone." I took a deep breath. "All you ever did was care about Charlie, and there's nothing wrong with that. I'm glad he had you in his life, and I know he was too. There's been a lot of times this year when I wished someone, like a grown-up, knew what was going on with my mom and stuff, but no one did. When I told my friends, they cared. And that made everything better, even if we had never found my mom."

Ms. Edgerly was quiet, and her eyes started getting kind of glassy. I wondered if I should leave. I didn't want to make anyone cry.

"I bet he'd be really neat and clean, too. He doesn't seem like a socks-and-underwear-on-the-floor kind of kid, if you know what I mean?"

Ms. Edgerly laughed and wiped at her eyes. "No, I bet he's not." She looked up at the clock. "Gym is almost over, kiddo. I'll write you a pass, and I will talk to Mrs. Verzoni about Finn's situation and see if there's anything the school can do."

My heart sank. I tried not to let the disappointment show on my face, but it was hard to believe that would mean anything more than a card signed by all his classmates and possibly a send-off party with a cake.

Maybe that was all the school could do. But I wasn't ready to give up on Finn; none of us were.

CHAPTER 40

"THIS WAS GOOD, DAD," I SAID, SCRAPING UP THE SAUCE at the edge of my plate.

"It came in a jar," Dad said. "The guy at the store said it was good on anything you grill."

"Better than spaghetti," I ventured, "or scrambled eggs."

Dad gave a short laugh. "Yeah, I guess I don't have what you would call a wide range as a cook."

"You tried something different," I pointed out.

Dad nodded, chewing his final bite.

"Hey, Dad," I said. "Do you think I could use the white shelf that's in Charlie's room?"

"For what?"

"I thought maybe I'd put it in the ice shack, maybe put some of my bigger Lego stuff out there. You know, like a little museum display."

Dad grunted. "Sure, I mean why not?"

We both sat with that for a minute. There wasn't a good reason. Charlie wasn't coming back for the shelf. None of us could go back. We could only go forward.

"You want some help moving it out there? Bruins don't play until eight."

Stepping into Charlie's room was strange. The air inside was still and empty. Most of Charlie's stuff was piled on his bed or the top of his dresser. The shelf, which he had cleaned off before he went to college, just had a few notebooks, his high school yearbook, and a handful of pens and pencils. I carefully moved these things to the bedside table.

The shelf fit perfectly in the ice shack, taking up the entire side of one wall.

We closed the door and stood outside in the cold, neither of us making the move to go back into the house.

"I saw some deer tracks out here yesterday, thought I might see where they go," Dad said.

"Cool," I replied.

"You want to walk with me?"

"Okay," I said.

We found the prints in back of one of the trailers near the Grove. Dad pointed out how to tell a buck's track from a doe's. We followed the tracks until we reached the road. The cold air made my eyes widen and water. When we got back to the Box, it felt warmer than before. I noticed that Dad had hung up a framed picture of the beach that Mom had bought a couple years ago, and that someone—Dad, I guess, since there was no one else—had finally turned the calendar on the fridge from November to December.

I went into my room and stood in front of the shelf that was overflowing with my Lego creations. Maybe I'd take the X-wing fighters out there or the *Millennium Falcon* I got for my birthday in fourth grade. I thought Dad had gone to watch the game, but suddenly he was standing behind me, looking into my room.

"You're good at that," he said. "Putting things together. You still have my old Legos?"

I nodded.

"You ever think about doing that Pinewood Derby? The one I did with Charlie. I bet you could make something really good."

"I think they only do that in Cub Scouts. I'd be too

old now," I said. But I wasn't trying to rub his face in it or anything.

"Oh yeah," Dad said. "Well, maybe we could build something together sometime."

"Okay," I said. "Well, Mr. Boudreau had this idea about making a mini-golf course here. It probably wouldn't be too hard to put together a couple holes."

Dad laughed and put his hand up to his head. "I bet he did. The guy's crazy about golf."

I was sure the next thing he would say would shoot the idea down, but instead he shrugged his shoulders and said, "Well, if he wants to front the money for materials, we could take a crack at it this spring."

I tried not to let the shock show on my face. This was definitely uncharted territory. Like I was feeling my way through a dark closet, unsure of where my fingers were going to land.

"My friend Finn has to move," I blurted out suddenly. It was a dare, really, or maybe a test. I was telling Dad something important to see how'd he react. I heard the sound of "The Star-Spangled Banner" coming from the living room. The game was starting.

Dad glanced behind him, but he took a step forward

into my room. "That the kid who lives in the group home?"

I sat down on my bed. "How'd you know?"

"It's been there for a while. I had a friend who lived there for a bit when we were kids. Parents used to fight something wicked. State would step in. He'd have to go live there or with a foster family for a while. They always got him back, though. Not sure if it was the best thing for him. He turned out okay. He's got the auto-body place out on Route One Hundred."

I nodded. "We're trying to find a foster family for him, so he doesn't have to move away."

Dad's eyes got wide. "Just you?"

"And my friends," I said.

"School know about that?"

"Kind of," I said.

"That's a big deal, Lucas. I don't know how much you should be involved in that."

I scowled. "Well, no one else is doing anything about it."

Dad stood up a little straighter. "We can't take him here, Lucas."

"I know," I said, but I could hear how sad my voice sounded, and I was mad about it. I didn't want Dad to see this part. "I wasn't going to ask."

"It's a good thing, what you're doing," Dad said. "Sounds

like something your mother would try and pull off. What do I know? Maybe you'll figure it all out." He ruffled my hair and left the room.

I sat there for a minute, unsure of what had just happened with Dad and feeling my hair slowly relax back down onto my head, my scalp still tingling from the touch.

CHAPTER 41

"HOW ABOUT A ROUND OF SARDINES?" ROBBIE ASKED.

We all stood up, got our jackets on, and walked toward the door. Robbie suddenly looked anxious and called out to me, "Hey, Lucas, can you help me find something?"

Robbie was a terrible liar. I walked back over to him, and he put his head down and whispered, "I need to talk to you."

"Okay," I said.

"Let someone else go first in the game and then we can talk."

It was all very obvious, but if Anna, Cat, or Finn noticed anything, they didn't mention it. Once we were in the woods,

Cat offered to hide first, and the rest of us split up to find her. Robbie charged off into the trees, and I figured that whatever had been so urgent, he had simply forgotten about it. But then, as I was looking for Cat behind a giant pine tree, Robbie jumped out, nearly scaring me half to death.

"Lucas!"

"Geez, Robbie!"

"Sorry, I didn't want anyone else to see us talking."

"What's going on?"

"It's my mom. She thinks we might be able to take Finn."

"What? Seriously? That's amazing!"

"It is, right?" Robbie seemed excited but he also looked worried. "She's looking into the legal part today. But she said she wants me to really think about it. Like she's making it partly my decision. Because, you know, it would mean another kid. There's already four of us, five if you count Pascal. It seemed like a really good idea at first. But it's also a really big deal." Robbie smiled. "She thinks it's fate. You know, because she always wanted another kid and Finn doesn't really have parents who can take him. I mean, he could have gone anywhere, but he ended up in our town, at our school."

I nodded. I tried to put myself in Robbie's place,

but I just couldn't. Dad was right about Mom; this was something she would have tried to pull off. Maybe before Charlie, maybe when *she* was a kid. But would it have worked? You could be a really good person and still not have things work out for you.

"Either way, you're a good person," I said to Robbie. I wasn't really sure why I said it, but it seemed like something he needed to know.

"Thanks, Lucas," he said. "I think we're going to do it. I just wanted someone to know I wasn't completely sure."

I shrugged. "My mom always says you're only ever about eighty percent sure of any important decision."

Robbie smiled. "Eighty percent, huh? That's pretty good. I think I can do that."

CHAPTER 42

WE WAITED UNTIL MATH CLASS. MISS LEGAGE KNEW WHAT
was up—in fact, I was afraid she was going to give it away.
She was talking about converting decimals to fractions, but
she had this silly grin on her face, and she kept looking
meaningfully at me or Cat or Finn. At five after eight, Anna
and I got called to the office over the loudspeaker. Sadie
Gillespie looked interested, but most of the other kids were
too sleepy to pay much attention. I found Anna and we
ran to her locker, where she pulled out a bag of acorn caps.

"I can't believe this is happening!" she said excitedly.

"I know."

"You did this, Lucas."

It was a nice thing to say, but she was wrong. "No, we

did this together. That's the whole point."

Anna shrugged and smiled. "Okay, so we start at Miss LeGage's door, right? I hope he doesn't step on them or like walk right over them or something."

"Finn's pretty observant," I said.

We laid out a trail of acorn caps, one every few feet, all the way to the conference room next to the main office. As we passed the entranceway with the trophy case, I looked up and smiled at Charlie's picture. Was this something Charlie would have done? Maybe. But I knew he would have thought it was cool. He definitely would have been proud of me. I looked at the picture of smiling Charlie and thought about all the different ways someone could be in your life even when they were really far away. Maybe I didn't have to shine exactly like Charlie, but I didn't have to live the rest of my life in his shadow, either. Anna cleared her throat and I walked faster to catch up with her.

Mrs. Belcher was in the conference room, and she had a big homemade cake decorated with the words *Welcome Home, Finn!* Marcus, Julia, and Alex were there too; they were blowing up balloons and then releasing them to fly all over the room with loud, sputtery farting noises. Cat and Robbie were taping a large banner to the back wall, while a very nervous-looking Ms. Edgerly was pacing around the room. Mr. Coughlin kept checking his watch as he stacked and restacked the paper plates and cups. Mrs. Verzoni was there, and she had managed to track down and invite Natalie. I had invited Dad, but he had to work and was kind of confused about why I wanted him to come to school for some other kid's party anyway.

Mr. Coughlin cleared his throat and called down to Miss LeGage's room to have Finn sent to the office conference room. Then we turned off the lights and waited. A few long minutes went by. Finally there was a light tapping on the door. "Come in," Mr. Coughlin called. I wondered for a second if this was too creepy—a dark room with your assistant principal lurking inside. But then the door opened, and the lights flicked on and we all yelled, "Surprise!" at a blinking and astonished-looking Finn. He scanned the faces, and I could tell he was trying to put the parts of things together.

"Finn," Mrs. Belcher said, "Robbie and I would like to know if you would like to come live with us."

"And," Ms. Edgerly added, "my wife and I would like to host you some weekends as well."

Finn blinked several times and looked slowly around at us. Impatiently Robbie blurted out, "You don't have to move! You can stay here with us!"

"Only if you want to," Anna said, a little more gently.

"I—I—I—" Finn stammered in a way that was completely un-Finn-like. "I don't know what to say."

"Wow," Robbie said, "Finn doesn't have any words? That's a first."

Everyone burst out laughing. When the room quieted down, a slightly more composed Finn found his voice.

"It's just that words fail me. Anything I could possibly say in the face of such a magnanimous gesture would be utterly inadequate."

"That's more like it," Cat said.

"How did you? Why?"

"Your kindness to others will be rewarded," I reminded him.

The side of Finn's mouth twitched a little bit. I couldn't tell if he was going to smile or laugh, but then the tears welled up in his eyes. "Let me cut some cake," Mrs. Belcher said, and the other adults got busy doing adult things like pulling out chairs and making conversation.

Natalie walked up to Finn and put a hand on his shoulder. "This is good, buddy," she said. Finn seemed to lean toward her, and his body softened. Then Anna walked over, and she put her hand on Finn's back, so we all did. We squished in together, and I thought about how funny it was, all of us crammed in there like some weird game-of-life sardines. Some kids get shoved out and some kids get squished in, and sometimes you have to make your own game and play it your own way.

ACKNOWLEDGMENTS

At the heart of any book I write are my students. When I wrote *Sardines* I had just taken a new job at a new school with a new grade level. I went from teaching eighth grade to teaching sixth and it was a bit of a shock to my system. Who are these children? Why are they awake in the morning, and why do they talk so much?

It was around that time that I found the kernel of this story and I asked my agent, Lauren MacLeod, if she thought I could write middle grade fiction. A word about literary agents; they're like good sports bras—giving you just the right amount of support to try new things while keeping you from flailing all over the place and looking ridiculous. Lauren is all that and more. I can't imagine my writing world without her. Lauren encouraged me to try writing for middle grade, and I'm ever so grateful she did.

I'm so glad this book found a home with Alexandra Cooper and HarperCollins. Thank you for helping to shape this story during such a challenging time, while working from home and parenting a toddler! *Sardines* benefited immeasurably from your excellent instincts and editorial wisdom. Thanks also to Allison Weintraub and the whole team at Quill Tree Books. Many thanks to Masahin Aleem and Cat Manning for the thought and nuance you encouraged and inspired me to bring to my characters. Thank you to Erwin Madrid and Catherine San Juan for the spectacular cover!

My favorite beta readers are teacher readers. I am so grateful to Kris White and Megan Blakemore—two of the earliest readers of this book who gave me invaluable feedback. I'm so grateful for my family and friends, who support me, feed me, laugh, and cry with me.

I finish where I started, with the kids. Each student I teach is a world unto themselves. I always wonder about those worlds, and so the story begins. Lucas's story is the story of any kid who feels like life has given them more than their fair share of challenges. It is the story of kids who are carrying around more in their emotional backpack than the adults around them may realize. Lucas's story is about the friends who help you shoulder the load.

I dedicated this book to my daughter, Eliana, and my son, Avi. Of all the wishes I have for them, the one I hold the most dear is for them to find the friends who will walk beside them, know them, and love them for who they are. A final thank-you to Lance for loving me exactly as I am and for always helping to carry the load.